Stories from Another Place

June Kingston Smith

ISBN: 1 876922583
ISBN-13: 978-1-876922-43-6

Linellen Press
265 Boomerang Road
Oldbury, Western Australia
www.linellenpress.com.au

Dedication

For Adam

Contents

Foreword

Stories from Another Place include some which have been published in The Society of Women Writers WA anthologies, published in newspapers and read on radio. Two have won first place in competitions. I hope you enjoy them.

June Kingston Smith

Acknowledgments

Thanks to my husband Robert for his love and support and thanks to Damon for his help with the cover and photo.

Sarah

It is New Year's Eve. Midnight is approaching and my anxiety is increasing. My mind is totally absorbed by those few seconds when the bells will ring in the New Year.

Will she come back this year? Will I see her lovely dark eyes gazing at me with love, black ringlets resting on pale shoulders? Ten years have passed since this century began – ten years and not one day without me missing her.

Such a wonderful, happy person, she charmed everyone. There had been many suitors, but it was to me she was betrothed.

Our parents had been friends for years and it was always expected we would marry, though it hadn't been expected we would fall in love.

I remember how excited she was, making plans for the house I bought for her and opening her birthday presents on New Year's Eve, her 20th birthday. My beautiful Sarah. Where are you?

It was bitterly cold that New Year's Eve when the old century died. Everything had turned white under a thick blanket of snow.

We gathered together for dinner, Sarah's family and mine, in my father's house. After the meal we sat in the comfort of the drawing room with its blazing fire, while Sarah played the piano and sang for us in her sweet, sweet voice.

Dressed in white lace, her dark curls piled on top of her head, she was an absolute picture, etched in my mind forever.

While she sang, her eyes found mine and I could see the happiness shining there. I felt the love between us swell in my chest and I longed for the day I could take her in my arms and call her my wife.

As midnight drew close we opened champagne and prepared to toast the new century – and our wedding, only one week away.

"Wait," Sarah said. "I will toast you afterwards. I must see the old year out and the new year in properly."

"No Sarah, not this time," I replied quickly, clutching her arm. "You mustn't. It's such a wild night and it hasn't stopped snowing. Forget it this year, my darling."

"Thomas, don't be an old silly." Her laughter echoed around the room. "You know I do this every year."

"Yes, I know, but it's freezing and you don't want to catch cold before our wedding, do you? Let it be."

"You are a worry, Thomas darling. It takes but a few moments. Humour me, my dear. We must start this year the right way. It will bring us luck." Sarah's smile was dazzling.

I looked helplessly at our families but they merely smiled, willing to indulge the whims of this delightful creature.

I suppose it did seem petty of me to deny her something she had done every year, but I didn't want that arctic wind howling through the house. It was bad enough listening to it whistling in the trees and rattling the windows.

"All right, Sarah. But please be quick." I released her arm and she giggled then stood on tip-toe and softly kissed my cheek.

"Thank you, darling."

Laughing, Sarah ran to the French windows. "Out you go, Old Year," she cried happily, flinging them open. The curtains billowed around her and flakes of snow fluttered to the carpet. Then, running excitedly to the front door, she waited, looking at me expectantly with smiling eyes.

As the grandfather clock began striking and the village church bells rang out, she pulled open the door. "Welcome, New Year," she laughed.

The wind gusted in, tearing at her hair, whipping her skirts, shrouding her in snow. She swayed unsteadily and as I reached for her she screamed. And was gone. As if into thin air.

"Sarah! Sarah!" I shouted, but her screams were faint, as if coming from a hundred miles away. A wet patch on the carpet was all that remained. The New Year had taken my Sarah.

Was I mad? Were we all mad? This was beyond belief. I am a doctor of medicine, not of physics or the mind, and I had no answers.

My family and Sarah's do not speak of this matter and my father has shut his house. He will not sell it, nor will he live there. But every New Year's Eve I go there at midnight and wait for the church bells to ring out ... as I am doing now, on this bleak, stormy night. Soon the bells will peal and I will throw open the doors ...

One Way Street

The news was bad. She had prayed for it to be otherwise, but when she saw his ashen face, panic gripped her.

"Three years ... I've got ... three years ... maybe more, if I'm lucky." His voice was slow and unsteady.

Three years! Oh God, three years! That wasn't long, not long at all. She saw him through a veil of tears, saw his set jaw and narrowed eyes. Her arms went out to him and he held her close.

"Don't cry, my darling," he whispered. "It ... it ... will be the best three years of our lives. You'll see."

They walked out into the sunshine. It was ridiculous. His arm was tightly through hers, steadying her, yet he was the sick one. But, as always, he thought of her before himself.

She blinked at the brightness of the day and wondered at the mockery of hearing such bleak news in this glorious weather.

"Let's stop at the river on the way home. It's too nice to be inside." Jim smiled at her.

Apart from his pale face, you'd never know, she thought. He seemed so composed. "Yes, alright."

There was a seat close to the water's edge and they sat down silently. He squeezed her hand. The sunlight danced patterns on the water and fallen leaves bobbed by like small boats. Jim watched them and said sadly: "That's how it is, isn't it? Life, I mean. The same as this river: we're all flowing in one direction, going forward to the unknown. Like cars going down a one-way street. They can't turn back and neither can I ..." His voice trembled and his shoulders began to shake.

Ann saw the tears on his cheeks. He crumpled into her arms and she stroked his hair and held him while her own tears also fell.

"Be brave, my love, and I will be brave with you," she said softly.

She never saw Jim like that again. Early each day he woke with a smile and whistled as he made his wife her morning cup of tea. And while she sat back in bed with her tea, he worked in his garden, weeding and raking, and tending his vegetables.

But Ann knew that, alone in one of his favourite places, he gave in to his feelings and cried bitter tears into the earth. There everything was living and he was dying.

"I feel like a round of golf today," Jim suggested one morning as he returned from his gardening. "It's a gorgeous day out there."

Ann nodded in agreement. "Good idea. The housework can wait."

The little golf course they used was adjacent to a large area of bush and parkland where Ann walked while Jim practised his shots. She didn't like golf.

She watched him, bent over the ball, deep in concentration. How many more ... but no, she wouldn't think about that. She had said she would be brave.

She paced briskly along the track she knew so well, breathing in the scent of the trees and enjoying the coolness as the sun disappeared above the canopy of branches overhead. It was peaceful, with only the sound of the birds whistling and chirping and the occasional buzz of an insect. In the distance she could hear the low hum of traffic on the highway.

She could be the only person in the world. It would be nice to stay here and pretend everything was alright, but eventually the track would lead her out into the sunlight, and reality, once more.

Ann's eyes searched quickly for Jim as she emerged and she saw his tall figure striding towards her. "We do have this down to a fine art," he laughed. "You always manage to come out of that bush as I get to this hole. If I get any quicker at this, you'll miss me." He squeezed her hand tightly. "Lunch?"

"Mmm, that walk has made me hungry."

"What about a pub lunch? I wouldn't mind a cold beer."

"Okay." They walked hand-in-hand to the car. "Did you enjoy your golf?"

"Yes, and I'm improving. One day I'll be really good, you wait. Might take a few years though ..." He stopped suddenly and she lowered her eyes so he wouldn't see the pain in them. He didn't have years! How easy it was to be lulled into a false sense of security, to forget that he was unwell. He didn't look at all ill. It just wasn't fair. Why Jim? He had never hurt anybody in his life. It just wasn't fair.

"Where do you want me to hang this?" Jim asked as he came into the room with his tools. "I'll put it up for you now."

He had bought Ann a painting for her birthday. "Oh, that makes a nice change. I usually have to wait for months," she laughed, but the laughter faded. Why did she say that? "Over here, above the chair," she added quickly.

"Good, it'll look nice there." He ignored her remark. "I'll have it up in no time. How about putting the kettle on."

Ann escaped to the kitchen and busied herself with cups and

saucers. She loved her kitchen — it was her haven, where she buried her troubles in pots and pans and baking.

She sighed. When Jim wanted to move from their home of forty years she was devastated. But he had been right. This little unit was cosy and small enough for her to manage, and there was a garden for Jim — not like he was used to, but big enough for him to grow his vegetables and some flowers. And she had never regretted the move. After all, retired people didn't need oodles of space. Only time ...

She took the tea outside to the bougainvillea-covered patio, where the chairs were set amidst ferns and lush green foliage, then returned to the lounge. "It's crooked," she smiled, her head on one side.

Jim looked down at her from the step ladder. "Is it now?" he chuckled. "Why don't you let a man finish his job?" He stepped down and straightened the painting. "There. What do you think, love?"

"It's beautiful." Ann kissed his cheek. "Thank you for a lovely present."

"You're worth it," he said, kissing her. "You're the best wife any man could ever hope to have." He pressed a piece of paper into her hand. It was a poem. He was always writing poetry for her.

She read it while he washed his hands. 'For my darling Ann,' it began. Her eyes filled with tears. How could she keep going this way? Falling to pieces inside while he seemed to be so calm. She just couldn't imagine what life would be like without him. She walked outside and sat down.

"It's ... it's ... you've written me such beautiful verse over the years," she stammered.

Jim smiled tenderly at her. "I love you, Ann."

It was a bleak, cold day, befitting Ann's mood when Jim went into hospital. She didn't cry. She was too numb.

The days passed – how many she didn't know. She walked with him in the hospital gardens, read to him, held his hand when he felt pain and sat by his bed while he slept.

"You'd better put my old typewriter away," he told her on the last day. "I won't be needing it anymore." And when she did, she found the poem, finished, but still wound around the roller. She released it and read the words: 'Memories of our Past'. Covering her face with her hands, Ann cried; cried all the tears she had saved over the last three years.

"Be brave," she said. And he had. He'd lived with the knowledge that there was only three years of his life left and they had used those three precious years, just as he said they would. Maybe the knowledge of how much time you had left brought with it a quality of life.

She felt empty and alone as she wandered into his garden and stood among the flowers. A little whistle startled her and she looked up to see a bird sitting on the fence watching her. It whistled again. A strange calmness suddenly enveloped her and she smiled. Ann wasn't alone in Jim's garden.

In Another Place

Rain pounded on the roof, wind rattled the windows and I was cold. So I put my soup on a tray and took it into the lounge.

Turning on one bar of the heater, I pulled my chair right in front and sat down. Much better. I found my patchwork rug and pulled it over my old arthritic knees. It was a great comfort to me, that rug. I remember when I made it – it took me ages, lots of nights in front of the fire, with Jack next to me reading one of his endless books. I never did understand most of them but he was such a brain; knew so much.

I finished my soup and picked up my knitting. Now where was I up to? Oh yes, the sleeve. I really should be doing this a lot faster but my fingers seem to be so stiff lately. Jack will be needing it now that winter is here. He does love the jumpers I knit for him, especially the blue one. He wears it all the time and I have an awful job trying to take it from him to wash. But he does look handsome in it.

A knock at the door interrupted my knitting. I rose slowly, waited a few moments for the feeling to come back into my legs, and hobbled to the front door. "I'm sorry to trouble you, Elsie love, but I just thought I'd better tell you there's a storm warning for later tonight. I wasn't sure if you knew."

It was May Sullivan from next door. She was a dear, always popping in to see if she could do anything. And she was very wet. "Thank you, May, I didn't know. My radio's not working."

"You'll have to let my Bern have a look at it, he's good with things like that. Now, we'd better take your hanging baskets down, you don't want them crashing down in the middle of the night, do you?"

"Oh no. Come in, May."

"Thanks, oh, can you smell something burning? What ... oh quick, look at your rug!"

May suddenly took hold of the rug and ran to the kitchen. When she came back she had a dark frown on her face. "Elsie! You'll have to be more careful or you'll burn your house down and yourself with it. Look at your beautiful rug, it's all burnt at this end. You must have let it fall near the heater when you got up to let me in. Now, now, don't cry, love. Here, use my hankie and wipe your eyes, it's clean. It's alright. It was an accident."

May patted my arm with her chubby hand.

I stared numbly at the diamonds on her short, thick fingers. Forever. They're stuck. She'll never get them off. She's lucky her Bern has given her so many rings. Jack only gave me a wedding band. It was all we could afford when we got married. He ...

"Elsie! Are you listening to me? Are you alright? I know it's upsetting, but I'm sure you can crochet another square onto it and then you'll never know the difference. Now, you sit tight and I'll go and put the kettle on, and take down your baskets. Oh, did you hear that thunder? This storm's going to be a beauty!"

I watched May go into the kitchen, and silence fell on the room again. She did chatter a lot, but a cup of tea would be nice.

"Did you say something, Elsie?" May's head appeared around the door.

"I was just saying a cup of tea would be nice."

"Oh. Won't be long then. You get on with your knitting."

"Alright. I'm trying to get this jumper finished for Jack. He'll be needing it with this weather coming on."

"Jack?" May's face appeared round the door again. "Jack?"

"Yes. I want to have it finished when he gets back from the country."

"Oh." May frowned. She did seem to frown and say 'oh' a lot.

The cup of tea was lovely and I sat with it on my lap after she'd gone. I could hear the wind howling through the roof and thunder crashing loudly. Lightning lit up the blackness outside and I hoped my Jack was safe.

The next day May came to see me again and she brought someone with her – a woman, very tall with red hair. She had it all piled up on top of her head and she wore thick-rimmed glasses.

"This is Mrs Hobson, Elsie. I've brought her to meet you."

I didn't like the way Mrs Hobson looked at me. She seemed to be looking right inside. "Hello."

"Hello, Elsie. It's nice to meet you. Hope the storm didn't bother you last night. It was quite a bad one."

"No. I don't mind when I'm tucked up in my bed." This person had a very prim manner.

"And what have you been doing with yourself today?"

"Oh mostly knitting this jumper for Jack." I held it up for her to see, but she was looking at May. They both looked back at me.

"Is Jack your husband?" Mrs Hobson asked.

"Yes."

"And … where's Jack now?"

"Why in the country, of course. He goes often – it's part of his job, you know. But he's usually only away for a couple of days."

"What sort of job has he got?"

"He's a salesman – takes boxes of clothes with him. He goes to all those little towns with no big shops, you know the ones."

"Don't you get lonely?"

"Yes. I used to go with him but now my legs are so bad I can't go anymore. But it's lovely when he comes home. I cook his favourite leg of lamb."

"That's wonderful, dear. Well, it was nice meeting you. Do you mind if I come again?"

"No, I like to have visitors."

"Alright then."

"Don't get up Elsie, I'll see her out, then I'll come back and make you a sandwich." May smiled at me.

"Thank you, May. I'll just get on with this knitting."

They moved to the kitchen door and I could hear May whispering to Mrs Hobson, but I didn't take any notice. I had wasted too much time and wanted to finish the jumper.

"Do you see what I mean, Mrs Hobson? She's convinced he's coming home."

"Yes. She's in a bad way, poor thing."

"Well I'm doing just about everything for her. She's so forgetful and she hardly cooks any more. I really am worried about her."

"Of course. I'll certainly do my best. The first vacancy, I promise you."

"Hello, love."

"Jack! Oh, it's good to see you. I've missed you so much."

"I've missed you too, my love. Here, let me give you a big hug."

"Mmm, that feels good. Look, I've got something for you." I held up the jumper and Jack smiled at me.

"Love, it's beautiful! As good as the old blue one! Do you remember it?"

"Yes, of course. You used to look so handsome in that one. Now, come and sit beside me and tell me all your news."

Jack pulled up a chair next to mine. He tucked the rug firmly around my knees and patted my hand. "You look very tired, my love. How've your legs been?"

"Not too bad. Could be worse!"

"Typical of you, Elsie. Never complain about anything."

"Jack, when can you take me with you?" I did miss him terribly.

"Soon, my love, very soon."

"Oh good. I do miss you, Jack."

"Elsie?" May's voice called from the back door.

"Come in, May. I'm in the lounge."

"Just called to see if you need anything," May said as she came into the room. She was dressed in a raincoat and boots.

"Oh, I see you're knitting something else. What happened to the jumper?"

"I finished it. Jack thought it was wonderful, too."

"Jack ... thought it was wonderful?" May stared at me, her eyes very wide.

"Yes. It looks lovely on him too."

"Is ... is he home then?"

"Yes, came home yesterday."

"Where ... where is he now?" May looked rather nervously around the room as if she expected to see him.

"Oh, he's not here. He's gone to the shops for me."

"The shops? Ah ... yes, I came in to see if you needed anything from the shops?"

"No thank you."

"Are you sure?"

"Yes, but thank you for asking though. Maybe you'll run into Jack while you're out."

"What? Oh, yes, maybe. Well, I'd better go. See you later then."

"Bye, bye." I watched May hurry from the room and wondered what had gotten into her. She was acting so strange lately. Maybe it was that time of life for her.

It was late afternoon and I was dozing off in my chair in the lounge when I heard May's voice again.

"Come in," I said, trying to wake myself up. I felt very tired. Must be all the knitting I had been doing.

"You really must remember to lock your door, Elsie. I've brought Mrs Hobson to see you again. Do you mind?"

"No, that's alright."

I sat up straighter in my chair and tucked my rug around my legs. They were really hurting today. I looked at my visitors and wondered wearily why Mrs Hobson was back so soon.

"May tells me that ... Jack is home." Mrs Hobson was smiling down at me. She seemed so tall.

"Yes. He came home yesterday. He loved the jumper too."

"That's nice, dear. Where is he now? I'd like to meet him."

"I'm sorry, he's not here."

"Not here? Where is he then?"

"Gone to the shops for me. I told May."

"But, Elsie love, that was this morning. He must be back by now." May was staring at me.

"No. He had a lot of business to do. Because he's been away, you know. There's always things to do when he gets home, bills and all that. You know."

"I see. What a shame! I would have liked to have met him before he goes away again. He ... is ... going away again, isn't he?" Mrs Hobson seemed disappointed. She would have liked Jack. It was a shame.

"Yes, he'll be going away again soon. But I'll be going with him this time."

"What do you mean, Elsie? ... going with him?" May, looking very pale, was wringing a hankie round and round her fingers. She really ought to see a doctor.

"Well, he said he would take me with him. I'm looking forward to it too. I want to be with him all the time. I do get lonely on my own."

"Yes, well, maybe you'd like to come and live with lots of other ladies like yourself. They'd be good company for you, dear." Mrs Hobson patted my hand. I felt like a little girl.

"I don't know. I like my house and I don't know if I'd like a lot of strangers around me."

"They won't be strangers. They're lovely people and they like knitting too. You could even swap patterns. And there'd be someone to cook all your meals."

"That sounds nice. But I'll have to see what Jack thinks. Thank you, Mrs Hobson."

"All right. I'll come back tomorrow and you can tell me. I know you won't be disappointed." She looked at May. "Maybe you can explain about the home." Poor May. She seemed so nervous. She kept looking from me to Mrs Hobson.

"Well, remember I may not be here. I'll be going with Jack."

"Ah, yes, Elsie, I'll remember, dear."

Mrs Hobson took May by the arm and as they left the room, I heard her say: "I'll come back tomorrow, May, and I'm afraid I'll have to take her with me."

"I know. What a terrible business! So sad."

"Yes, but it's the only way."

But it wasn't the only way. Jack came back for me and said I wouldn't have to be alone any more, or live with strange people somewhere else. I could stay with him forever. In another place.

Won The Society of Women Writers (WA) Bronze Quill Award 1986.

The Diary

She stands outside the neat brick house and sighs. It's not going to be easy. It never is. There is something unnerving about going through somebody's personal things.

Walking to the front door, she pauses, keys in her hand, wishing her grandmother would open it and greet her with that beautiful wrinkled smile. But no, that would never happen again. Things were different now. Everything was different.

The door squeaks noisily. Inside it is dim. Musty. Shafts of sunlight escape through chinks in the heavy closed curtains and make dappled patterns on the carpet.

Linda draws back the curtains and opens the window. Memories crowd her mind, jostling for position as she looks around the room. The chair next to the bookcase is empty, waiting. But the old lady will not return. A book is lying open on the floor next to a pair of spectacles. They had fallen there when ...

Tears fill Linda's eyes. She picks up the spectacles and slumps into the chair. Her grandmother had loved her books and was reading right to the end ...

"Gran ... why? Why did you have to go just when I need you most? I need you to listen and tell me what to do. There's no-one else I can talk to." And she cries until there are no more tears.

When Linda stirs from the chair the room is dim once more.

The day has gone and darkness is filling the room. She shivers. There is a cold breeze coming through the window. Moving as if in a dream, she closes it and draws the curtains, shutting out the world. Now there is only herself and a houseful of shadows.

Switching on the lights, Linda walks to the bedroom and empties the contents of the dressing table drawers onto the bed.

She looks at the assortment of underwear and lace handkerchiefs and wonders just what she will do with them. Then she sees the book – a thick book covered in brown paper with a picture of a red rose on the front. Gran loved red roses.

Linda opens it. A diary. A very old diary with well-thumbed pages, and the year 1920 on the first page:

He is wonderful. So handsome and very tall, with dark hair and a lovely big moustache. I can't believe he likes me.

Linda feels the tears behind her eyes as she reads the fine familiar writing.

I never realised what it means to be in love, and be loved in return. Edward has asked Father for my hand in marriage, and Father has agreed. I am so happy. I am the envy of all my friends too. I suspect they might be in love with him as well.

Edward! Linda's eyes move to the wedding photo hanging in its walnut frame above the bed. Two very happy, beautiful people stare back at her. Edward and his bride, Dorothy.

Being married is better than anything else in the world. Edward is so gentle and considerate and I never dreamed lovemaking could be like this. It's not like Mother told me at all. I feel like I am living in the clouds.

Linda thought of her own marriage to Ed, the man with the same name as her grandfather. He too was tall and good looking, and she had been the envy of her girlfriends when she married him. And he also was gentle and considerate, and very loving.

She marvels at the similarity and then winces. The similarity ended there. Her grandparents had been married for 60 years, while her own marriage … … she lowers her head as another entry catches her eye:

I am so miserable and unhappy. I cannot believe this has happened to me and I have no-one to talk to. Mother wouldn't listen anyway. Some say that it is a normal thing for a man to do and a wife should not mind. But I do. I can't stand the thought of my Edward, my beloved Edward, with another woman.

Another woman! Linda shivers as she feels the pain of her grandmother's unhappiness and misery.

"Oh Gran, I know. I know what you're going through." She looks again at the smiling groom in the photo.

It was only one night, but that makes no difference. He has betrayed me after all our promises to each other.

"My poor Gran!"

He says it meant nothing, that it should not have happened. But I don't understand how he could do this to me.

"I don't either," Linda whispers. "But he did it just the same. Told me it meant nothing too, but I don't believe him. One night or ten nights, it makes no difference. It all comes down to the same thing. Being unfaithful! And Ed was with that person who called me 'friend'."

I have sent him away. I cannot bear to have him near me. He told me she seduced him but I don't want to hear any more. He cried and said he loved me more than anything and didn't want to lose me.

How easy it would be to put my arms around him, but I mustn't. He must pay for what he has done. Our marriage is over.

"Ed told me those things too, Gran, but I've left him. Oh how he pleaded with me not to go, telling me how much I mean to him. But it's too late now."

I am so desperately miserable and I don't think I can stand much more. I miss my Edward and I feel so confused.

"Yes Gran, I understand. I do love Ed, even after what he did. It's so unfair. To be so happy one minute and the next, so sad and empty." Linda cries and the tears fall onto the already stained and yellowed pages.

I cannot go on any longer. Life was not meant to be this gloomy and bleak, I am sure. I cannot live without him. These past six months have been like an endless convict sentence and I have done nothing wrong. I must go to him.

"Gran! You can't do that! He must come to you and ask to be forgiven."

Pride is a terrible thing, and I have been guilty of it for too long. I am only twenty and I cannot stand the thought of my life passing without him. I mustn't punish him forever. He is suffering too. I know because my friends have told me. I must be proud no longer.

"I suppose you're right. It's awful to be so proud, but it seems wrong that you have to be the one to go to him ... and yet ... if he is suffering too, and is too proud to come to you, you will never be reunited."

My life has begun again. My dearest husband was so repentant and pleased that I had gone to him, my heart melted. It is not in me to be so cruel. I love him too much. And I know he does really love me.

Our married life will start from now. The past is over and done with and will never be spoken of again to anyone.

"Oh Gran, you were so right. You had such a happy marriage and Grandpa was so thoughtful towards you. He worshipped you. I remember so many wonderful things about him and I never dreamed you had gone through all this. How can you have been so young and so wise?"

Linda brushes away the tears with the back of her hand. "Ed."
The name is whispered. She looks at the ring on her finger.
"Thanks, Gran. You've never failed me."

And she closes the diary.

Won the International Training in Communications (ITC) Australian Pacific Region Fiction Writing Award 1996.

Rest in Peace

I'm lying here dying. I can't speak but I can hear you all saying how sad it is that I have this disease because I'm so young and such a lovely man, caring for my father until he died. Wouldn't hurt a fly ...

It was late in the day when she walked into the deserted cemetery. Shadows were lengthening and leaden clouds scudded across the sky. A cold wind whipped at her long mane of blonde hair as she wandered among the graves, occasionally stopping to read a headstone.

Beneath the spread of an angel's wings she read aloud the words chiselled into the stone. "Resting in Peace. Sam Pontifex, 1935-1965. Mmm, even the dates fit. Sam, I like your name, you don't mind if I take it do you? After all, you don't need it any more. You're dead."

Thunder suddenly reverberated across the darkening sky and lightning forked through the clouds. She stood, pulling her flapping coat around her. "Thank you, Sam," she murmured, and hurried away as heavy drops of rain began to fall.

Sam stepped off the coach and lowered her two suitcases to the ground. Across the road a two-storey timber hotel with its huge wrap-around veranda beckoned. Adjusting her shoulder bag, she hefted up her cases and walked over to the entrance, but as nobody sat at reception she dropped them and went through to the bar.

Silence descended as she entered. One by one everyone stopped to stare. Smiling, she approached the man behind the bar. "Hi, I've come about the barmaid's job."

"Who wants to know?"

"Sam … Sam Pontifex. You are?"

"Steve Hilton." His blue eyes travelled over her tight jeans and cropped white T-shirt.

"When you've finished looking, is the job still available?"

"Yeah, it is. You experienced? In bar work, that is."

"Yes, I am."

"References?"

"No, sorry … they … were destroyed in a fire, but I could work a day for nothing, then if you're not happy it's my loss."

"You from the city?"

"Sometimes. I go where the wind takes me."

"Is that so? And it brought you here, did it?"

"Seems as good a place as any. Now, what about my offer?"

"Okay, a day for nothing."

"Thanks, and I'll need a room too. My cases are at reception."

"Go back there and I'll get Jeanie for you." Steve disappeared through a door behind the bar.

Sam watched a huge woman barrel down the hallway, her purple dress billowing around flopping blue thongs.

"Hello. Steve told you I'd work for a day for nothing?"

"Yeah, but I own this place and I 'ave the final say." Jeanie's frizzy black hair framed her weathered face with its slash of red lipstick.

"Oh. So what is your say?"

Jeanie looked over the desk at her. "No problem." She pushed a book across the counter. "Name and address." Sam signed her name and passed the book back to Jeanie.

"Address?"

"Here. My address is wherever I am."

"Drifter, eh? Yeah, we get a few of those. Secretive lot." She snapped the book shut. "'Ere's your key. Up the stairs, left and room 13 at the end of the passage. 'ope yer not superstitious. Ladies' bathroom's next to it. Breakfast at eight and you start at ten. Steve will show you the ropes."

"Okay, thanks."

At the end of the following day, Sam put away the last of the glasses and sank with a sigh into a chair. "What a busy night. I didn't know this town was so bloody big."

"There's more to this place than the main street. Lots of people live out on farms or near the timber mill just out of town, and a lot of guys would've come in to check you out. Word travels fast around here." Steve smiled, sat on the chair next to her and passed her a beer.

"Right. Well, how'd I do? Am I hired?"

"Yeah, you're hired, you're a bloody good worker. Speak to Jeanie tomorrow and she'll let you know about your wages. Meals and lodging are included, so it's a pretty good wicket."

"You live here too?"

"Yeah, my room's just along from yours." He gave her a wink. "Been here ten years. It's a not a bad place to live."

"Married?"

"Nope. You?"

"No ties."

In her room, Sam brushed her short bob, leaning forward to stare into the mirror. *Yes, black hair suits me. Knew it would.* As she replaced the brush on the old wooden dressing table she felt a sudden pain in her temples, and a vision of a woman with red hair and blue eyes, mouth open in a silent scream of terror, flashed into her mind. Images of heavy bush followed – a line of gum trees and a big old tree with an unusually shaped, burnt-out cavity at its base.

Within a few seconds the images disappeared, leaving Sam's head throbbing. Finding some aspirin, she gulped them down with a glass of water and lay on the bed. *Where did that come from?* It had never happened before. She turned off the light and pulled the faded chenille bedspread over herself.

As she began to drift off, Sam suddenly felt she was not alone. Sitting up, she switched the light back on. *Nothing.* But the feeling persisted. She walked to the window and looked out. A couple of street lights illuminated an empty street. *You're just tired*, she told herself, going back to bed. *That's the first full day's work you've done in ages and you're tired.*

The following day Sam decided to explore the main street in her break. Apart from the hotel, there were a few shops and a town hall, which was next to a park, where she stopped and sat on a bench.

Nice town. She could get to like it, though usually something always happened to make her move on. But no, not this time. Hadn't she changed her appearance, taken a new identity? A new life? Her old one was gone. Joanne Taylor and all that was connected to her was gone. Things were going to be different now.

As she stood, the stabbing pain in her temples returned. This time she saw a blonde, face contorted in pain, mouth wide and silently screaming, followed by the image of the trees. Sam clutched her head between her hands and sucked in air. *Go away, just go away!* As the pain subsided she again felt that someone was there. But the park was deserted.

Hurrying back to her room, she found the aspirin, swallowed two with water and lay on the bed, head throbbing. *What's going on? What is happening to me?*

"Sam, Sam! You in there?" Steve's voice woke her. "Sam!"

"Stop shouting, I'm here." She opened the door and glared at him. "What's bloody wrong?"

"That's what I'd like to know. You're an hour late from your break. What's going on?"

"Oh, oh hell. I'm so sorry. I had such a blinding headache I just had to lay down. Steve, I'm so sorry."

"Okay, it's lucky for you we weren't busy, but Jeanie wouldn't be pleased if she knew. C'mon, straighten yourself and come down."

"Thanks," she touched his arm lightly. "I really appreciate this."

"Yeah. How's your head?"

"Well, the throbbing's stopped. Just a dull ache now, but I can live with it. I'll be down in five minutes." She smiled at him and closed the door with a sigh. *You can't let this happen again*, she told herself. *If you want to stay here, get a grip.* Sam changed her skirt, fixed her makeup and hair. *No more headaches, everything's going to be okay.*

But two days later the pain stabbed at her again while she washed glasses at the end of the evening. Dropping the glass into the sink, she clutched her head. "No! No! Go away!" And there was another woman's face, dark hair, huge frightened eyes, mouth wide and screaming, followed by the trees.

Sam sank to the floor as the throbbing began and the feeling of being watched returned. She looked fearfully around, but the room was deserted. Steve had taken the rubbish out to the bins and left her to finish the glasses. As she sat there she knew there was someone next to her. She shivered, suddenly feeling threatened.

Scrambling to her feet, she backed away. "Keep away from me, whatever you are. Go away! Just bloody go away!" The feeling of evil persisted, but when she heard the back door slam, it was gone.

"You okay?" Steve said as he saw her standing against the wall. "You look terrible. What's happened?"

"I … I don't know. I …" How could she explain? "I'm alright. Really." She just couldn't lose her job. Not now.

"Sam, come here. Sit down." Steve gently pulled her into a chair. "You don't look alright. Here," he poured her a brandy, "drink this. It might help."

She gulped at the liquid, felt it burn her throat. "Thanks."

"Is this another headache?" He sat beside her and covered her hand with his.

"Yes, yes it is." She stared at him, at his lovely blue eyes and curly blonde hair. Would he understand what was happening to her?

"Are you sick or something?"

"No, I've just been getting a lot of headaches lately."

"For how long?"

"Since … since I've been here. But Steve, I really want this job …"

"Okay, I understand. We won't tell Jeanie about it, but I'd like to help. We have a doctor in town."

"Thank you, but I'll see how I go."

While she was getting ready for bed at the end of the second week, Sam had her fourth vision, another blonde, and the overwhelming feeling of something threatening her. With her head throbbing and tears she could not control, she threw open her door and ran along the hall to Steve's room.

"Steve, Steve!" She banged her fist on his door. As he opened it she fell into his arms.

"Sam, what's wrong? What is it?" He pushed her from him and stared at her. "What's wrong?"

But she couldn't speak through her sobs. He held her close, stroking her hair. "It's okay, it's okay."

"Steve," she choked, "I have to tell someone. I know you won't believe me, but I don't have any friends, no one else I can talk to."

"Look, sit down, I'll get you a drink, or would you like a cup of tea or something?"

"No, no. I just need … to talk right now. I … I don't know what's happening to me." Sam slumped into a chair; pushed her hands through her hair.

Steve pulled up another chair in front of her. He reached out, cupped her chin with his hand. "Tell me. I'm listening," then leaned back and watched her.

"I've … been having visions."

"Visions?"

"Yes, when I'm alone. I have stabbing pains in my temples and a vision followed by a violent headache and … and … a feeling that someone is watching me. Each time I have the vision, I feel more and more threatened. Whatever it is … it wants to kill me. I just know it. Steve, I'm not making this up. Nothing like this has ever happened to me before and believe me, I've been through a lot."

"Ssshhh, Sam, it's alright. Tell me about the visions?"

"First I see a woman, a different one each time, always screaming, though I can't actually hear anything, but they are all terrified. Then I see lots of bush with gum trees in a row … one has an unusual hollow at its base, sort of burnt out. But … but each time I have the vision, the feeling that someone is watching me is more intense."

"Do you know these women, or recognise the bush?"

"No, I don't know who they are. Oh Steve, please believe me. I know it all sounds weird and you don't know me or anything but tell me I'm not going mad."

"I do believe you, Sam." He ran his fingers gently down her cheek, wiping away the tears. "And I don't think you're going mad. This is just a little timber town. Some people have lived here for years, others drift in and out. I was a drifter once, and we all have history. I don't know about your past but it's your future I'm worried about."

"Steve, I'm so bloody scared."

"Sam, you … you're not on drugs, are you?"

"What? No. I … I … did do drugs when I was 15, but I've been clean for years now. You must believe me."

"Why do you think I don't?"

"Because … because, oh it doesn't matter. But I'm not lying, and I am scared, terrified really. Why am I suddenly having these visions?"

"I don't know." Steve stood and moved to the wardrobe where he pulled a blanket from the top. He wrapped it around her shoulders.

"Thanks." Sam suddenly realised she was only wearing a T-shirt. "I'm … I'm sorry, I should go and let you get some sleep."

"Sam, do you really want to go back to your room?"

"I … yes … no." She looked at him, her large eyes filled with tears. In two strides he crossed the room and pulled her into his arms.

"Stay here then." Sam stared up at him. She needed to trust someone. And she wanted it to be him.

For the next week Steve rarely left Sam's side. He stayed with her during the day and she stayed with him during the night. He was gentle and considerate and asked no questions. Gradually she relaxed, enjoying his company. It was so good to be living a normal life.

"Sam …" Steve appeared from behind the bar with a bag of rubbish. "I've just got to take this out the back and lock up and we're done for the night. Do you want to go on up or wait for me?"

"I think I'll go up – I'm shattered. It's been bloody busy today."

"Okay, won't be long. You can warm the bed." With a wink and a grin, he disappeared.

He was such a gorgeous guy, she couldn't believe her luck.

Sam trudged slowly up the stairs. After all the men she had known, he was certainly the best. A clap of thunder made her jump as she entered Steve's room. She turned on the light, quickly pulled the curtains across. God, she hated storms.

As she sat on the bed the pain returned. Sam covered her face with her hands, saw a woman's face contorted with fear, her long red hair a thick mass of tangled curls. Suddenly, as lightning flashed into the room she felt the presence, intense and menacing. Eyes wide with terror, she sat paralysed.

Thunder boomed. A chair hurtled across the room. Pictures rattled on the walls and the wardrobe doors flew open; banged shut. Slammed backwards into the wall, Sam remained pinned by an unseen force, pressure on her throat preventing a scream. A trickle of blood ran down her blouse.

Faces of the women in her visions floated in front of her eyes. She heard their voices now, feminine and fuzzy, as if from a long way off. They were crying and repeating a word: Dan … Dan … Dandenongs.

A terrifying sound, an inhuman growl, echoed around the room. Sam smelt the decaying stench of her attacker's breath on her face, felt the evil closeness of him. She heard someone hammering on the door, tried to scream, fought desperately to pull away from the invisible hands pinning her to the wall. Pressure increased on her throat. She couldn't breathe. Then everything went black.

Steve heaved his shoulder at the door. Fuck! It didn't budge. He heaved again and again until it finally flew open, sending him sprawling into a freezing room. He shivered as he stumbled to his feet, hardly daring to believe the nightmare he had entered.

The faces of five terrified women swirled in a mist in front of him while a menacing roar reverberated around the room.

Halfway up the wall, arms and legs spread out, blood streaming from the claw marks on her face and throat, Sam stared at Steve through blank, unseeing eyes. He threw himself at her, tried to pull her down. He smelt the fetid breath, felt it on his neck and as he turned something clawed at him.

"You bastard," he screamed, struggling to free himself. "Whatever you are go back to hell where you belong! Dear God in Heaven send him back. Please Holy Jesus, save us, take this thing away." Tears streamed down his face as he continued his losing battle. The women's faces still floated around him, but now their voices joined in his prayer. "Jesus save us. Save us."

Sam suddenly fell from the wall and Steve landed heavily beside her. Thunder shook the window, shattering the glass, letting in a howling wind that tore at the curtains and hurled furniture around the room. He pulled her to him, held her close. Then it was quiet, the storm gone.

"Sam, Sam, talk to me." But she didn't move. He heard a low murmur, saw the faces again, floating in a mist, smiling now. With a soft sigh they slowly disappeared.

Sam's eyes fluttered open. Steve was sitting beside the bed, holding her hand. She tried to speak, but her throat hurt too much.

"Shhh, baby, don't try to talk. You're going to be okay. Everything's okay." He bent over her and brushed his lips across hers. "Sleep, Sam, you need to rest." Sam closed her eyes, his words melting over her like honey.

"You need to tell me about Sam Pontifiex."

Sam sat opposite Steve at the kitchen table, her hands fiddling with the lid of the teapot between them. She looked at him with wide eyes. "Yes, yes I do. You are the only person I have ever trusted who hasn't let me down. I know I owe you an explanation."

She was tired of running, tired of always trying to start a new life and, most of all, tired of being alone. Now she had a chance for a new beginning. She had to tell Steve the truth, had to trust him that little bit more if she wanted her new beginning to be with him.

"Are you ready to tell me now?" Steve reached across the table and covered her hands with his.

"Oh bloody hell yes. I was born in Queensland and my mother dragged me to every state in the country. I don't know who my father is and I trusted my mother until I was five. Then I realised what sort of person she really was. I trusted a couple of my "uncles" too, until they decided they liked little girls.

"I've spent my life rebelling against everything. I've been in foster care and institutions and even spent a short time in jail for stealing. Everyone I've tried to get close to has let me down one way or another. In recent years I've just lived on the streets in Melbourne.

"I drifted until it all became too much for me. Nothing ever seemed to work out. One day I sat with a knife at my wrists but I just couldn't do it. I knew I had to get away, right away. If I began somewhere new, changed my looks and name, then maybe, just maybe, I'd have a chance to live a normal life, find a place to call home.

"I burnt everything that belonged to … to Joanne Taylor and searched for a new identity. I thought a complete new beginning as far away as possible would be a good idea. That's why I decided to come over here to the west, and I found this little town tucked away in the bush where nobody would know me.

"But, before I left Melbourne I … I found myself in a cemetery and … and …" Sam's voice faltered as she thought about the horror she had unleashed.

"Sam babe, it's okay. It's all over." Steve moved around the table to pull her to her feet. Putting his arms around her, he pulled her close. "It's over."

"But I can't stop thinking about it. I … I remember looking at his grave and thinking what a good idea to take someone else's name. Steve, I don't know how I've survived all this. It seems like I've just lived in a bloody horror movie."

"Yeah, real nightmare stuff and I can't quite get my head around it either. But you've survived because you are a survivor, otherwise you would have given up and you would have used that knife. I've drifted too, near-marriages, broken relationships, something always going wrong. I'm a survivor too."

"Steve, I'm so lucky to have found you. I don't ever want to hear Sam's name again, the thought of it makes me shudder."

"Well, you weren't to know you'd picked the name of a bloody serial killer, one who had killed five women and got away with it, one who almost killed again. From his grave! The police will be scratching their heads over your visions for years. You've given them five graves up in the Dandenong Ranges, and the name of their killer. You've solved the crime and given the families closure, and those poor women are now free. You're free. He can't possess you anymore. He's history."

"Well, I certainly don't want to be Sam Pontifex any more, but I don't want to be Joanne Taylor either."

"Okay. How about Irene?"

"Irene? Why Irene?

"It's the name of my grandmother. I lived with her until she died when I was 12."

"Oh. Okay, that's a nice name. But Irene who?"

"How about … Irene Hilton?"

"What are you saying? That … that's your name."

"Yes. Marry me and we'll both start new lives. Together. Here."

"Here? Do you think we'll still have a job, especially me?"

"Leave that to me – I'll take care of the damage. What do you think?"

"You *are* too good to be true! How can I turn down an offer like that?"

"You can't. After what we've just been through I think we can survive our future life together."

"I think we could survive anything now." Sam kissed him. She had finally found her place to call home.

Escape

The Governor slammed his fist on the table. "He must *not* be released! Ever!" He sank heavily into his chair. "Don't they understand?"

"No. No I don't think they do." Murphy heard the desperate frustration in his boss's voice. "In view of the fact they never found any bodies and there wasn't a lot of evidence, the Board is definite about his parole in two years."

"Then they are fools! They don't know what they're dealing with."

"With respect, Sir, what *are* they dealing with?"

"None of you know him like I do." The Governor leaned forward and stabbed a finger into the desk top. "That man is evil – pure evil. He will never be anything else."

"If he is that bad, why haven't they been able to find more conclusive evidence? He has such a clean record. Surely someone so evil couldn't be so good."

"I know it doesn't make sense to you, Murphy. Sometimes it doesn't to me, but I believe … I *know* …" The Governor shook his head and pushed back his chair. Turning to the window, he gazed down at the exercise yard. "He's down there. Look at him. No wonder he has you all fooled."

Murphy looked over his boss's shoulder. "What were you going to say? What do you know?"

"You can't feel it, can you?" The Governor's face was inches from Murphy's. "You just can't feel that sense of evil when you're near him." He sat down again. "*He* knows I know and he also knows I can't do a damn thing about it. Nobody would believe me."

"What do you know? What *are* you talking about, Sir?"

"Have you seen the books he reads? No? Well, I'm telling you … he can … make things happen …"

"I don't understand …"

"No, of course you don't. Neither does anybody else. He's only been here a few days but I have known him for some time and I guarantee any trouble that happens in his block will be caused by him. Yet there is no way I or anyone will be able to prove it."

"Do you mean hypnotism or something?"

"More like 'or something'. Take it from me, that man is not what he seems. There are only two ways out of this prison – through the gates or in a box – and I'm going to make certain he doesn't go out through the gates!"

"What are you drawing?" the warder asked, squinting through the bars. "You're always drawing."

"I'm not drawing, I'm painting." The man smiled as he set down his brush.

"Same difference," the warder sniffed. "But I wouldn't call that a painting, all them purples and greens. Ain't natural. Wouldn't hang it on my wall."

"Well, it's not going on *your* wall. It's going on mine."

"No accounting for taste."

Smiling, the prisoner stood up and held the painting at arms' length. Jagged fingers of purple rock thrust upwards through a forest of dense tree tops, like silent fortresses shadowing green hills, which gently rolled to a sheer drop of purple cliffs. From three of these fingers a board protruded, reaching out over the cliffs, a diving board to nothingness.

"Like I said, no accounting for taste," the warder said. But there was no reply. The prisoner was staring into the painting, the smile still playing at the corners of his mouth.

"Sir, there is trouble in S Block." Murphy's voice was agitated as he held the phone with shaky hands. "You'd better come down here right away."

"Right, Murphy, I'm on my way." The Governor's footsteps echoed around the damp stone walls as he strode through the cold corridors of the prison. As he reached S Block he felt the hairs stand up on the back of his neck and perspiration trickle down into his collar. He wiped his clammy hands down his trousers. The noise was deafening, but the riot was over and the men were being ordered back into their cells.

"Well, Murphy? Who started this?"

"I ... I don't know, Sir."

"Take me to *his* cell! Now!"

"Yes, Sir."

"Where is he?" the Governor demanded as they stood staring through the bars at the table with its tidy stack of books and paint brushes, the neatly made bunk, the pictures taped to the walls.

"I'm ... I don't know." Murphy looked incredulously at the locked door.

"So how do *you* account for this?" The Governor rattled the lock.

"I … I …"

"That painting, that abstract there … what is it?"

"I … don't know. He was always painting. It's awful, isn't it, Sir?"

"Murphy, open the door! Open it!"

He fumbled with the key and stood aside as his boss strode into the confined space of the missing prisoner's cell and peered at the painting. "Look at this!"

Murphy's face drained as he too stared at the wall. "Oh my God!" There on one of the boards looming out over the strange purple cliffs was the figure of a man dressed in prison uniform. And he was smiling.

Old Tom

We always enjoy our winter holidays at Spender's Mill but as I watch the rain teeming down outside, I am reminded of the last time we visited that tiny mill town.

The day we left, our station wagon loaded with food and bedding and the twins squished somewhere in between, there was a terrible thunderstorm. The rain was relentless, pounding our car for the entire three hour journey and putting me in a mood as bleak as the weather.

But it stopped as we arrived in the late afternoon and we were glad to stretch our legs and breathe the clean, fresh air of the bush, the familiar scent of wet leaves and musty undergrowth filling our nostrils and making us grin at each other. Our tedious journey was behind us and our holiday ahead.

My mood soon changed when we discovered there had been a mistake in the bookings and our usual cottage had gone to someone else.

"Don't worry, the one next door is empty and it has been cleaned," the caretaker, Essie Harrison, told us. "I'm sure you'll like it just as much."

Reluctantly we moved our gear inside and Jerry gravitated towards the wood stove. Every year it was his job to look after all the fires, and there were three, including the chip heater in the bathroom. But the flue above the wood stove was broken. "Never mind, if you can manage tonight, Bill will fix it in the morning," Essie placated us with a smile. Nothing fazed these country people.

So I heated some of my homemade pies in our electric frying pan and we sat in front of a crackling open fire in the lounge, listening to the rain hammering on the iron roof while we made plans for our stay.

The following day after Liza and Peter, rugged up in their parkas and boots, had gone off to find Old Tom, the Harrisons arrived with the new flue which they managed to fit with little trouble and less mess.

By the time the twins returned, I had the kettle on and some scones (albeit out of a packet) in the oven. Jerry and I were ready to relax in front of the fire. But Peter's expression soon changed that idea. Old Tom was missing. And Spender's Mill without Old Tom just wasn't Spender's Mill. A knot formed in my stomach. "Have you looked around? Maybe he's at the shop."

"His shack is empty and he's not at the shop. They haven't seen him today."

"Well, he's probably out walking somewhere. You know how he loves to walk through the bush," Jerry said soothingly. "Don't worry, Pete, he's as tough as old boots."

"But, Dad, the place looks so empty. There's no sign of him and we're worried."

I removed the scones from the oven, putting them to one side along with my thoughts of a relaxing day, and found my boots and jacket. "Come on, I'm sure we'll find him."

As the four of us tramped through the rotting leaves and mud on the path to Tom's shack I thought about our first holiday at Spenders, five years before. While out walking we had seen the old man picking beans in his garden. Peter, then a 10-year-old chatterbox, had presented him with a barrage of questions. Apparently Tom normally avoided people, but for some reason he talked to us for some time.

Over the years we became friends, much to the astonishment of the caretakers who themselves barely knew him, and the twins really looked forward to visiting him.

Old Tom had been the sole survivor of the town, which had been built in the 1920s by the Spender family. After it closed in the 1970s, the mill, deep in the heart of the karri forest, had been bought by an enterprising businessman who renovated the empty cottages and rented them out as holiday homes.

No-one knew much about Tom, except that he had always been there. Many years before, after the death of his wife, he'd moved from his cottage and built a shack deep in the forest, where he retreated with his memories.

The shack, old and decrepit now, seemed small and insignificant beneath the huge trees. The enormous branches stretched out in a protective canopy above, while the leaves made whispering sounds in the wind.

"I'll never understand why he chose to build his shack here," I said with a shiver. "It's so eerie."

"Yeah, I agree." Jerry squeezed my hand. "Bloody silly, I reckon. He should've stayed in the town, especially now he's older."

"But, Dad, he loves the bush and I think he's happy to live here in solitude with his memories," Liza said.

"I know all that," Jerry nodded. "But it's still not right. I mean, look at him now, out here, God only knows where. If he stayed in town the caretakers could keep an eye on him."

"Well, maybe," Liza replied, knocking on the door. "Tom,

Tom, are you there?" But all was silent as they pushed open the door of the empty shack.

"C'mon." Jerry pointed to a narrow track leading past the wood heap. "Let's see if he's down here."

"Oh, I wish we could find him," Liza said, frowning. "I just know there's something wrong."

"Don't worry, love." I put my arm around her. "We'll find him."

The rain began to fall silently as we followed Jerry along the track, but because of the thickness of the branches above us we were offered a measure of protection. However, a chilly breeze found its way through, causing the leaves to continue their whispering.

"It's so quiet," I said nervously. "The birds aren't even singing."

"And cold," Jerry added, pulling up his collar and jamming his hands further into his pockets.

Suddenly Peter shouted, "Look, over there! It's Tom!" He pointed to a fallen tree where a figure sat huddled amongst the dead branches.

"Tom! Tom! It's me, Peter." But Tom sat motionless, as if in a trance. "Tom, are you alright?" Peter put his arms around the old man.

"It's twenty years," he said in a thin, frail voice. "Twenty years."

"Come on, Tom, let's get you home." Jerry tried to pull him to his feet, but he refused to move.

"Twenty years," he muttered to himself. His tattered jacket was soaked and his ancient trilby sat at an angle on his head with water dripping off the brim onto his nose.

"C'mon, old fella," Jerry said gently. "We'll soon have you home."

"Twenty years ago my Annie left me. Right here."

"Here?" I asked, puzzled.

Tom looked up then gazed at me with pale, sad eyes which moved towards the tree. "Yes, right here. An awful storm … lightning … it … fell on her. Killed …her … but her spirit is still here. Can't you feel it?"

I stared anxiously around me, not knowing what to expect. The rain was still falling and the wind was still moving through the trees. Yes, I could feel something. Scared.

"You *can* feel it, can't you? I know you can," Tom said urgently, and I didn't know whether it was tears or rain on his face. I glanced at Jerry.

"We've got to get you out of this damn rain. How long have you been here?" Jerry patted his shoulder.

"Don't know … maybe … all night. Annie … Annie was calling."

Jerry and Peter managed to get him to his feet but his body was cramped and he winced with pain. Eventually we got him back to his shack and into bed, while the twins were sent to phone the doctor.

"I'm surprised that this place is so tidy," I said to Jerry as he stoked the kitchen fire and the warmth began to fill the small room. It had a table, two chairs and an old stuffed armchair next to the fire. Beyond was an even smaller room where Tom lay in his bed. "What do you think happened to all the things he must have had in his house when his wife was alive?"

"I don't know. Strange, isn't it? He certainly doesn't have much here."

"I wonder if he ever gets lonely."

"He's a recluse. I don't think they get lonely. God, I wish those kids would hurry back. Just listen to that thunder, and it's pelting down. I hope they're okay."

I listened to the wind whistling through the roof and felt the draughts coming through the cracks in the walls. How could Tom ever survive a winter in this dreadful shack? I suddenly felt an urge to be back in Perth in the comfort of my lounge room.

"How's Tom?" Peter burst into the room, dripping and breathless.

"Sleeping. Where's Liza?" Jerry answered, an urgent note in his voice. "Is she okay?"

"Yeah, she's waiting at the Harrison's for the doctor." Peter held out his hands in front of the stove. "Do you think he'll be alright?"

"I don't know, Pete," Jerry said slowly, handing him a mug of steaming tea. "He's too old to be out all night in this weather."

"But he's a nuggety old thing, Dad. You said he's as tough as old boots." Peter moved towards the bedroom. "Tom, please be okay," he whispered, gazing down at the still form.

"Is that you, Peter?" Tom's eyes opened.

"Yes, Tom. How do you feel? We found you out there in the bush. What happened?"

"Annie … Annie called."

"Annie?" Peter looked at me and I shivered.

"I think he's delirious," I said quietly, tears pricking my eyes.

"Annie called," Tom said again. "I went to her tree … and … I tripped. Right at her tree. She didn't want me to go, you see. I couldn't get up." His eyes moved towards an old cupboard next to his bed, on top of which was a tiny antique clock and two picture frames. A woman looked out from one, a child from the other, alike, yet different. Tom pointed to one and Peter picked it up. "My Annie. She wants me to come now."

"She's very pretty, Tom," I said, trying to control my tears. Peter put the photo back on the cupboard. "Who … who is the child?" I asked.

"Mary," Tom said simply, and closed his eyes.

We all breathed a sigh of relief when the doctor suggested that after a few days in bed Tom should recover, providing his chill didn't turn into pneumonia. But suggestions of hospitalization brought an outburst from Peter. "He'd hate it; he'd die there. I can look after him here."

"Well, as much as I don't want to admit it, I know you're right," I agreed. "But this is hardly the place for him to get well. He could die here too."

"But if he stays in his bed, I can keep the stove going and you can make him some soup. I'm sure he'll make it."

"Well, I …"

"Please Mum, he'll die, you know he'll die."

"I know. I'm sure between the four of us we'll manage."

"Well, Mrs Canning, if you're sure you want to spend your holiday this way, thank you. I'll call back tomorrow, but if his condition worsens, he will most certainly have to go to hospital, whether he likes it or not. Just keep him warm and make sure he takes his medication every four hours."

"We'll look after him, Doctor." Jerry extended his hand. "Thanks for getting here so quickly."

"No problems," Dr Whyte smiled. "Old Tom is very lucky

you found him in time. He's a strange one, but harmless enough."

"Do you know much about him?" I asked.

"A little. Why?"

"Do you know how his wife died?"

"Yes. She was lovely, so gentle, and had an affinity with the bush. Tom had trouble keeping her home – she walked in all weather, day or night. And then she died in it. A freak accident during a storm – a bit like the one we're having now – about twenty years ago I think. Lightning struck a tree and it fell on her, killing her instantly."

I gasped, feeling my blood drain. "And … do … do you know anyone called Mary?"

"Ah, Mary. She was their only child and he adored her as much as his wife. She was a pretty little thing too, but she disappeared when her mother died. Ran away, I suppose, and Tom was devastated. She was only twelve and was never found. He left his house and came out here. Are you feeling okay, Mrs Canning?"

"Yes," I murmured. "It's just that … he's been talking about his wife … Annie, and then Mary." I couldn't bring myself to tell him why Tom had gone to the tree; it was hard enough for me to understand.

As the days passed, Tom lay motionless in his bed, muttering the names of his wife and daughter, while we kept a constant watch over him. But he made little recovery.

The stormy weather abated for two days then returned with even more fury than before. Thunder rumbled and lightning forked in a heavy sky.

"This is one of the most amazing storms I've ever seen," Jerry mused, standing at the lounge room window. "That lightning is fantastic."

"Yes, and look what it did to Annie. I'm scared Jerry. I want to go home. Just about everyone else has gone."

"C'mon, love, don't be frightened." He put his arm comfortingly around me. "It's just a bad storm, and we *are* on holiday."

"It's not just a bad storm. This weather is from the devil himself. It's the worst we have ever seen, like an omen or something …"

"Cassie, love, don't talk like that. There's nothing to be frightened about."

"I want to go home. This holiday has been a fiasco from the start."

"No it hasn't …"

"The weather was bad the day we left – it took us hours to get here, crawling along with our headlights on. Then the cottage was wrong, then no stove … and Tom! Don't forget Tom!"

"I'm not forgetting Tom. If we hadn't come on this holiday he would have died. Do you realise that? No-one would have found him. They wouldn't have even missed him."

I looked at Jerry, stunned. I hadn't thought of that. That poor old man would have died out there in the bush. He had no other friends, no-one to look out for him. I felt so selfish.

"And while he's so sick we can't leave. We promised to look after him," Jerry added, squeezing my shoulders.

"You're right, love," I sighed, sitting down near the fire. I looked up at him. "I don't want to think of Tom lying out there for days …" The tears ran down my face and Jerry kissed them away.

"The twins will never regret this holiday, you know that," he said. "Despite the outcome … they'll come back."

"I know."

"Well, I'm going to see how they're doing. Coming?" He began to pull on his boots which had been drying near the fire.

"Yes."

Jerry opened the door and was confronted by a steady stream of water pouring through a hole in the veranda roof. "Got your umbrella handy?" He said wryly. I smiled grimly as I side-stepped the leak and looked out at the bleakness of the day.

The sky was almost black, illuminated at intervals with lightning flashes. The rain was slanting down, almost horizontally with the force of the wind. We were wet through before we reached the front gate.

Jerry took my hand and smiled as we made our way to the edge of the forest and I suddenly felt comforted. I had my family, no matter where we were.

The majestic Karri trees now looked like savage giants with arms extended, creaking and moving in the wind as they beckoned us forward. They enveloped us as we hurried through the sludge and mud on the forest floor but at least the rain wasn't quite as drenching as it fell through the canopy of branches overhead.

A brilliant streak of lightning stabbed the sky and we saw the old shack ahead: it sat in its dilapidated state, battered by the rain with the wind wrenching at the flapping, rusting sheets of iron and rotting timbers.

"My God," I cried, "the place looks like it's going to collapse! They can't stay in there!"

"No, absolutely not, but God knows how we'll manage Tom. We can't bring him out in this."

I pushed the door open and felt a blast of warmth from the

stove. At least it was warm inside.

"I was just coming to get you," Peter said anxiously, emerging from the bedroom. "Tom's had a terrible night."

"He hasn't stopped talking about his wife and Mary," Liza added from behind him. "Mum, I think his mind has gone." She began to cry. "He keeps calling for Mary and asking if I'm her."

"Don't cry, pet, it's okay. Tom's very ill but he'll pull through." I put my arm around her, wishing I could believe my own words.

"I don't think so, he's so weak." Peter's voice quivered. "I think he's dying."

"Well, let's go and see." Jerry forced a smile. I knew it distressed him to see our children upset. "The doctor is due any time now."

"Yes, but what if it's too late," Liza whispered in a choked voice.

Tom lay staring at the ceiling. "Tom," I said softly.

"Mary? Mary? You've come." Tom's voice was shaky and faint."

"No, it's Cassie." I looked helplessly at Jerry who shrugged. Tom didn't move, just continued to stare at the ceiling, as if waiting for the wind to rip the iron from the roof.

"Tom, would you like some tea? Or soup?" I patted the worn, wrinkled hand which rested on the faded bedspread.

He turned to look at me with eyes glazed and distant. "Annie said Mary would come. Can't go before I see Mary."

"Annie? Mary?" I asked slowly, goose bumps forming on my skin.

"Annie told me Mary would come before I go."

"Where is Mary, Tom?"

"Don't know. But she'll come. Annie said."

A clap of thunder suddenly reverberated through the forest and lightning flashed through the dimly lit room. The lamps flickered.

"She's here," he whispered.

I stared at him, but he was looking past us, towards the door.

We turned to see a slim woman, with long black hair clinging wetly to the olive skin of her face. Large liquid brown eyes watched us. She carried something in her arms, wrapped tightly against the weather.

"She told me to come," she said softly, laying the bundle against Tom's chest.

A smile flickered faintly on his creased face. "Mary?"

"Yes. And I've brought Thomas with me. See?" Mary pulled some of the wrapping away from the bundle to reveal the tiny, dark face of a perfect little baby.

"Thomas." Tom's hands caressed the baby gently. "Thank you, Mary." And, with the smile still on his face, he slowly closed his eyes.

The Man Who Built the House

Henry Wilson was a quiet man who lived a quiet life as an only child with his parents. Since his school days he had been in love with Gloria Raymond but she didn't know. He was too shy to tell her. His mate from his school days, Johnny Brown, offered to tell her for him but Henry said no, he would do it himself.

Gloria, also an only child who lived with her widowed father, worked in the local store and was in love with Henry. But she too was shy. Her friend Daphne said she would tell him as the situation was driving her mad. But Gloria said that wouldn't be right. She would wait.

With the threat of war looming, Henry, who was a carpenter, decided to build a house. His parents' old house was on an acre of land and they offered part of it to him. They were fed up with their son's shyness and hoped, at the age of 22, he would build the house and summon the courage to ask Gloria to marry him.

Every weekend Henry worked on his house, sometimes with Johnny's help and sometimes with his father's. Slowly it took shape. There was a veranda across the front with wooden pillars he carved himself, three small bedrooms, a bathroom with bath and basin, a kitchen with a wood stove, sink, two cupboards and a table and chairs, as well as a lounge room. Outside he built a small wash house and a toilet.

"You've done yourself proud, son," Henry's beaming father said. "It's a great little cottage."

"It's turned out better than I expected. I just need to put some linoleum on the floors and I think I'll put a fence around the place, just to separate it from yours."

"Good idea. Let's go and find Mum. She's been desperate to have a look."

"What's your next plan then?" Mavis Wilson asked speculatively as she stood in the middle of the lounge. "You can't let this lovely house sit here empty can you?"

"I have plans, Mum, don't worry."

"Well, if you don't ask Gloria to marry you soon you'll miss out, she's such a pretty little thing. And with this war, who knows what will happen." Her son never did anything in a hurry, no matter how much prompting he had.

"Yes, Mum." Henry shook his head, smiling.

But the war came to Henry's town and, before he had time to think, he was in the army. Johnny urged him to speak to Gloria. "Mate, I know she's waiting for you to say something and this might be your last chance."

"No, I can't. If I make it out the other end of this war I will talk to her, but I'm not going to do that to her now. It's not fair to her."

"Bloody Hell! That's bloody stupid. She needs to know you care about her."

"No, I might not come back, or I might return without a limb. *That* wouldn't be fair to her." But Henry thought about Johnny's words and made his decision.

Gloria accepted his proposal of marriage without hesitation. She had waited so long for him to declare his love she didn't want a courtship.

"I've built a house, and it's waiting for you to turn it into a home when I return and we marry," he said. "Let me show you."

The night before Henry left for war they slept in his house. His heart and soul were in it, he told Gloria, in the wooden walls, the iron on the roof and the boards under the linoleum. He had put everything into this building, ready to make it a home for them. "This is my gift to you," he whispered. "The heart of this house is beating for you. I will return."

"But I'll not live here until you come back, my love, then we will start our life together here."

But Henry didn't return. His body lay shattered on the battle field, the name 'Gloria' on his dying breath. He didn't know that, at the moment of his death, Gloria also died giving birth to their daughter. And he didn't know that Gloria's father named his granddaughter Gloria before he too passed away.

So baby Gloria was adopted and taken to Queensland to live with her new parents. And the house waited. And is still waiting …

My Mother's Captive

Te big black stallion hurtled along the bridle path, his rider leaning forward, cape flying, urging the animal on through the still dark night …

"Leanne! Leanne!"

She was calling. Again. When would she ever go to sleep? I threw down my pen, my chair scraping the floorboards as I pushed it back in disgust. What now? She had water. She had been to the toilet. What else was left at this time of night?

"Coming," I called with exasperation as I stamped up the stairs. "What's wrong this time?" I opened her bedroom door and switched on the light.

My mother was sitting up, her short grey hair sticking up in spikes, her tiny dark eyes piercing me with hate from her wrinkled face. "I'm cold, but what do you care? Scratching away down there with your silly stories. I want another blanket."

"I do care, but I've been up here five times already. Look, here's another blanket, now go back to sleep." I tucked her in as she slid down in the bed. "It's late. You should be sleeping." *And my stories aren't silly.*

"You don't care about me. You just want me to die!" That would be a good idea, I muttered as I shut the door. "Why don't you leave the door open and stop shutting me in here?" She was really getting to me now. I turned back angrily and pushed the door open.

"Why don't you stop bullying me?" I yelled. "I've been looking after you for years when no-one else will and what thanks do I get? None. That nursing home is looking pretty good."

"You won't put me there!" My mother struggled to sit up. "You won't get a penny from me if you do," she wheezed.

"I don't want your money. Give it away, give it to the cats' home, I don't care. I just want you to care about what I'm doing for you." *And some peace and quiet would be nice.*

"You're my daughter, it's your duty. Anyway, I don't know what you've got to complain about … you've had free board all these years, living under my roof."

"Yes, free board and a happy life," I sighed. It was no use arguing with her. The fact that I'd given up a perfectly good job and an apartment five years ago just to look after her made no difference. It was expected. I was an only child and she refused a nursing home, using my inheritance as a lever. It was important to me once, now it isn't. I've had enough of her domineering and her bullying. There's no love between us. I don't really think there ever was. I should put her into a home and get my life back – what there is left of it – and the inheritance can go to hell. I slammed the door and ran down the stairs.

Since I gave up everything for her my life seemed to be on a downward spiral, full of washing and housework and cleaning up after a demanding and thankless mother. No time for socialising or even dating, that would be nice. I was at her beck and call and it was taking its toll.

My Dad died years ago – driven to an early grave I suspect – and I left home at nineteen to get away. The promise of a large inheritance and guilt for abandoning her brought me home when she became ill. Now all I want to do is leave but I am a prisoner, my mother's captive. I can't just walk out.

However, in the middle of all this misery I discovered an escape. Writing. Every spare minute I write – stories, articles, anything. I just escape into another world. And now my world is my novel. A romance, of course, because I don't have one.

Amelia is my beautiful heroine and she lives in London in the 1800s. She is engaged to Frederick, a very staid lawyer, but Nathan is the character who supplies all the action and intrigue. At six feet tall he is broad shouldered, with dark hair curling about his collar and eyes as blue and deep as the ocean on a summer's day. A full, sensual mouth and aquiline nose complete his handsome face.

Very much a ladies' man, he doesn't concern himself with whose wife he is bedding and has few morals. He is part of the King's court, and when not chasing women he gambles and occasionally works on his estate. Amelia is secretly in love with him and eventually I might give him to her. Sometimes I don't quite know what to do with him.

When Nathan makes love to a woman I am completely lost in what I write. The words seem to appear by themselves on the page as if I am not even in control. I dream about him when I go to bed at night, of him making passionate love to me and rescuing me from this life to take me to another.

"Leanne! Leanne! Where are you?" My mother again. What could she possibly want now? I stare at my notes longingly. A love scene and she calls me. Trying to ignore her I keep writing but the voice doesn't stop. Demanding. Accusing. I cover my ears with my hands and concentrate on Nathan. *Go to sleep, just go to sleep. For once leave me in peace.* "Leanne! Get up here now! I need you!" *You need me to lock you away.* I shoved my chair back so hard it toppled over. Ignoring it, I ran angrily up the stairs and flung open her door.

"What?" I screamed. "What could you possibly want now?"

"I'm not feeling well. And don't scream at me. Where's your respect?"

"It's gone, Alma. A long time ago."

"And don't call me Alma, I'm your mother. Now get me something for my pain."

"Yes, Alma." Anything to shut her up.

Finally she is quiet, due to the sleeping pill I gave her instead of a painkiller. It's two in the morning but I'm not tired. My head is full of ideas and my hand is flying across the page as I write. I can hardly keep up.

Nathan has ridden through the night to visit his latest conquest. Oh Nathan, why aren't you riding into my life? A hero to rescue me and set me free. But these things only ever happen in novels, never in real life.

"Leanne?" A voice. Not my mother's. In my head? It sounds so close. So soft. "Leanne, turn around." And there is Nathan. My wonderful, gorgeous Nathan. And I'm definitely dreaming. But when his arms go around me I know I'm not. So I must be going mad. I knew my mother would do that to me eventually. "Leanne, you're not dreaming. I am here. You have given me life."

"How?" My mind is struggling to deal with the fact that he has just walked from my pages into my lounge room.

"I don't understand how but you are always on my mind. I can't stop thinking about you."

"But … but I think about you too … because … because I created you. I created you in my novel. This … this isn't possible."

"Well, it must be, because here I am. I was compelled to come. I have ridden long through the night. I need to be with you and I know you need me too." Nathan pulled me to him and his eyes locked with mine. I was suddenly lost in the blueness of them. And then he kissed me. Well, if I created him and he is now standing before me, and my mother is finally sleeping …

I moved off the bed and found my dressing gown as if in a dream. Looking back, I watched Nathan stretch, his lean body, naked under the covers. "Leanne, you are so beautiful." Me? I don't think so, but then, I *am* the writer I suppose. My predicament now is what to do with my lover. "I would do anything for you," he said. "I owe you my life." *Mmm, now there's a thought.*

"Let me make some tea and we can discuss it," I laughed. "Just stay where you are."

"Leanne! Leanne!" *I don't believe it.* I should have given her the whole packet of sleeping pills. "I'll be back," I whispered. "Don't move."

"What's wrong, Alma?" I stood in the doorway glaring at her.

"I heard voices. Have you got someone in your room?"

"Chance would be a fine thing. Who could I possibly have in there at this time of night?"

"I'm not sure what you get up to when I'm sleeping."

"Well, an orgy or two would be nice, but you hardly ever sleep, and I don't have time to get up to anything with you summoning me every five minutes. Close your eyes and rest, it's almost time for your breakfast."

"Yes, well I want eggs on toast and mind you don't burn the toast like you did last time. And don't make the tea too strong. I like it milky."

"Your wish is my command." I bowed and slammed the door shut. What I wouldn't like to do to her!

"Your mother is not a nice person," Nathan said when I returned to him with our tea.

"That's an understatement. Did you hear all that?"

"Yes. I wish I could help you."

"Maybe you can," I said thoughtfully, sifting through all the ideas bouncing around in my head. "Maybe you can."

I sat at my desk, pen poised over my story, while Nathan lounged on the sofa, long legs casually crossed, watching me intently.

"Does she ever come down stairs?" he asked.

"No, she can barely walk, let alone manage the stairs. She would probably fall ..." My sentence remained unfinished as he caught my look. "Do you still want to help me?"

"Of course. As I said, I owe you my life." He stood up. "I will return shortly," He smiled as he walked towards the stairs.

I was busy writing when I heard a scream and a loud thud. I rushed into the hall where I saw my mother in a crumpled heap at the bottom of the stairs. I looked up as Nathan came down and stood in front of me. "She's had a fall," he said simply and walked into the lounge.

I followed him and put my arms around him." Thank you," I whispered and kissed him. He sat back on the sofa, rested one arm along the top, casually crossed his legs and watched me through half-closed eyes as I picked up my pen.

The shots rang out through the forest but only one man fell. The small group of men gathered around the body, murmuring, while the man holding the gun watched. "That's the last duel you will fight and the last woman you will lust over Nathan Hartfield. Damn you to Hell!"

I looked at the sofa and saw the dent in the cushions where Nathan had been sitting. "My life for yours," I said out loud. I picked up the phone and dialled for an ambulance.

A Renovator's Dream

When we first saw the house I heard its voice. "I'm your house, I've been waiting for you." But we drove by. It wasn't on our 'houses-to-look-at' list and it was getting late in the day. Time to go home and feed the kids.

Back at our rented house we fed and bathed the baby and two little ones, settled them into bed then sat down to eat our own dinner.

"This house-hunting has got knobs on," Charlie grumbled as he forked up pasta.

"Oh I'm sure we'll find something soon," I answered, sounding more confident than I felt.

"Do we really have to go out again tomorrow? The kids will be pretty irritable by tomorrow night after two days of driving around looking at boring houses."

"Well, we'll promise them a trip to the park on the way home."

"Mmm, what will you promise me? I'm going to be irritable too."

"I'll cook you something nice. But, seriously, we do need to go out again. We only have the weekends together and we're running out of time before our lease is up."

We had moved to Western Australia from Queensland three months before. It had been a sudden decision on my part but as neither of us had family ties there, and Charlie was so easy going, he agreed with me, though he couldn't understand why I chose

Western Australia. I couldn't either, really.

"Yeah, I know. I suppose I'm kidding, but you love doing this more than I do. Anyway, we have to go back to the area near that old house and look at the houses we missed viewing today. They're open again tomorrow."

"I would like to check that old place out while we're there. It's strange, but I feel drawn to it and it's been on my mind all night. I can't stop thinking about it."

"You're joking! I bet they've advertised it as a 'Renovator's Dream' too. More like a renovator's nightmare if you ask me."

"Maybe, but I do want to have a look. I should have written down the number that was on the 'For Sale' sign."

"Don't worry, we can do that tomorrow as we drive past. Quickly!"

The next day we viewed the remaining houses on our list but they weren't suitable for our family of five so on our way back we stopped in front of the old house.

"I know you're itching to have a look so I'll stay near the car to keep an eye on the kids while you have a wander," Charlie said. "And watch out for snakes," he added with a chuckle.

"Thanks," I laughed as I tentatively pushed open the gate which was hanging hopefully by one hinge to a picket fence. Well, I think it had *been* a picket fence.

The house was on a large overgrown block but it looked solid enough, weatherboard with an iron roof and a veranda with carved wooden pillars across the front. The garden had long ceased to be a garden and was now more a jungle where I would probably find the Phantom and the pygmy Bandar, as well as a snake or two, so I stayed carefully on the cracked concrete path that led from the broken gate to the front door. I don't know why I knocked as the place was deserted, but it seemed the right thing to do, though I suspected it hadn't been lived in for years, if ever. I looked through a cracked window but it was like trying to look through a blanket, it was so dirty with dust and cobwebs. The house seemed lonely, unloved and sad, and as I stood looking at it I had the strangest feeling it was again saying: "I'm your house. I'm here waiting for you." Suddenly I knew it was going to be ours even though I hadn't even been inside. Charlie was going to think I was mad.

Well, he did think I was mad, but as I am the love of his life and he is a wonderfully talented handyman, we bought it (at a much reduced price) and moved in. Then our work began. Amazingly there was little termite damage, but peeling paint and wallpaper, broken windows and linoleum glued to the floorboards were horrendous jobs which we had to wedge between Charlie's work in insurance in the city and me looking after three children under four.

But we managed. We repaired windows, stripped wallpaper, painted, and pulled up the linoleum which revealed wonderful wide floorboards, which we polished. We even knocked down walls and added some new ones, and when our new kitchen arrived in a box Charlie put it together. We painted all the walls white and I made curtains. Charlie bought a chain saw and tackled the jungle which soon reverted to a garden, complete with fish pond, chooks, a baby goat, three cats and vegetables. The house suddenly seemed vibrant and happy. If that's possible for a house.

Charlie's parents had died in a car accident and as my adoptive parents were also dead and we had no siblings, we really didn't know anyone in our new state. However, we made friends among our neighbours and time passed happily until we decided to move. The country beckoned and the kids, now at primary school, thought living in the south-west would be fun — swimming at the beach, horse riding, walking through the bush, and freedom. So we bought a house in a lovely little town and decided to rent it out until we were able to organise everything.

Months went by and we still hadn't moved, nobody wanted to buy our house. Then Christmas came and went. Eventually, two years later, Charlie and I finally made up our minds. Now or never. But our oldest two, Evie and Matt, were devastated. They were about to start high school and the thought of starting over in a completely new school had no appeal whatsoever, neither did the horse riding, or the freedom. So we sold the house in the country and I almost heard our old house whisper its thanks.

A year later I fell in love with a house closer to the city, where I now had a part-time job. It was bigger than ours and only required some touching up. I persuaded Charlie it was a good idea so we put our house on the market again but there were no offers. Finally a builder arrived and decided it would be a good investment as he could sub-divide our block and make some money. But when we phoned the agent of the house we wanted to buy he informed us it had just been sold to a cash buyer. Did I imagine it or did I hear a soft murmur echo around our house?

Not long after I found another house with renovations already completed and it was gorgeous. The agent told us the owners were on holiday and nothing could be done until they returned in a couple of weeks but by then they changed their mind about selling. I couldn't believe it. How hard was it to move house?

Within six months another house came on the market, also closer to the city. We wanted to put in an offer but the agent told us an offer had already been made and unless we could come up with a cash deal in two days we would lose it. Which we did. Our house didn't sell.

I decided to take matters into my own hands and after the new owner of the house moved in I knocked on the door. It was opened by a woman with a small girl clinging to her leg. She was the cutest little thing with a mop of red curls and a pair of fairy wings attached to her sparkly T-shirt. I introduced myself and explained that I was the person who had missed out on the deal but was still interested. "If for some reason you decide to sell, please phone me first." I wrote my phone number down and handed it her.

"Well I don't really think that's going to happen, Gloria, because I'm recently divorced and this little munchkin here and I have fallen in love with this house. But I promise I'll keep your number. Just in case."

A year later she phoned me. She had met someone and they were going to live in Victoria so would I be interested in buying the house before it was listed. My heart did a flip. Then sank. Charlie and I had just used up a great chunk of our savings to take our family on a holiday to Europe for two months. As we were leaving the following week there was no way we could afford buy the house, let alone sell ours.

What was happening? We had missed moving to the country and missed buying three houses in the suburbs. "This is weird, Charlie. It seems as if our house is not letting us go. We'll never move."

"Don't be silly, Gloria, of course we will. We'll find something else, you'll see."

And we did. Evie and Matt had moved out and Liam was thinking about it when I found a villa, ideal for the two of us. It was quite new and really only needed freshening up. Wonderful. But once again we were thwarted when our house didn't sell, despite our best efforts at showcasing it. Then I heard a soft murmur, the whisper of a breeze through the house and Charlie heard it too. "I think you're right, Gloria honey," he said. "I don't think our house wants us to leave."

The years have passed, the kids have married and had kids of their own, and we're still here, and are meant to be here, I'm sure. After all, we have had a happy life with our family and friends, and there are memories everywhere we look (even the growth chart marks we left on the bedroom walls), and as we have both retired we don't need to be close to the city anymore. Besides, despite all our efforts to move we really do love the house. It was so sad and neglected when we first saw it, ready for demolition we were told, and we made it happy.

So, because we never knew the background of our house and I now have time, I decided to do some research. Delving into its history revealed the owner, Henry Wilson, had built it for his sweetheart before he went off to fight in World War II. Sadly he never returned. As he hadn't married it had remained empty for years, though we couldn't understand why his girlfriend didn't live here. But eventually a distant relative was found in England and ownership transferred. Even then it had been on the market for months, defying demolition, waiting for us. If the house had arms they would be firmly around us, holding tight. And we're happy to be in its embrace. We know now that we'll be here forever. We can't leave. Not that we want to anymore. This house was waiting for us.

Ghost Dog

L ight drizzle began to fall as I swung off the main road into the lane, my headlights piercing the darkness. I hadn't planned on being this late to my new house, but the traffic had been horrendous, and now it was dark. My real estate agent gave me directions when I picked up the keys, telling me it was the only house at the end of a short lane and I couldn't miss it.

As the house loomed amongst the trees, I slowed down and parked the car in front of the gate. Using my phone torch I made my way to the front door and tried the keys in the lock. The door opened and I found the light switch.

I was standing in a narrow hallway with doors leading off from either side, so I decided on a quick tour of the house before bringing in my things.

Doorways to three bedrooms and a bathroom were in the hallway and a doorway at the end led to a lounge and kitchen/dining room with a laundry on the back veranda. The house appeared to be in good condition and the furniture looked okay.

Initially, I was a little concerned at renting a furnished house unseen for three months, but on paper it seemed exactly what I needed, a quiet place to finish my novel by the deadline that was looming.

The agent told me the previous tenants had done a 'moonlight flit', taking only their clothes and personal things, leaving the furniture behind. After failing to locate them he had finally decided to keep the furniture in the house, in lieu of the rent that was owing.

I turned on the gas heater I found in the lounge and went back to my car to retrieve my luggage. A movement caught my eye and I saw the pale shape of a large dog sitting under a shrub near the front door. Startled, I stopped, wondering if he was friendly but he loped away and disappeared. Not a good night for a dog to be out, the rain was becoming heavier. I zipped my jacket up and, pulling its hood over my head, grabbed what I needed for the night. The rest would have to stay in the car until morning.

Later I sat in the lounge with a mug of hot soup and some crusty bread I had brought with me and thought about how I would manage my time here. Tomorrow I would have a look around to get my bearings and check out the shops, which, apparently, were a couple of kilometres away. Hopefully it wouldn't be raining so I could walk.

I cleared away my dishes and headed for the bedroom – I chose the larger one as there was a gas point where I could connect the heater from the lounge and a window overlooking the front of the house. There was also a small desk in one of the other bedrooms which I could bring into my room and place under the window for my laptop and documents.

Now tired after my long journey I made up the bed with my linen and listened to the rain drumming on the metal roof as I fell into a deep, dreamless sleep.

The next morning was cold but the rain had gone, so after bringing in the rest of my luggage and unpacking everything, I set off to explore.

The house was enclosed by a picket fence. The lawn was well kept and there were a few shrubs and a lemon tree laden with bright yellow fruit, which I could definitely use. An old, empty tin shed sat at the back of the property near a gate opening onto a path leading into the bush surrounding the house.

Going around to the front of the house I opened the gate and walked down the lane I had driven on last night. A sign at the main road pointed to Regan River, two kilometres away. As I began my walk into town, I caught a glimpse of the dog again. He was a big white Samoyed and was sitting under a tree watching me. I stopped walking but he disappeared into the bush. Surely he wasn't lost, he was so beautiful.

Regan River was a delightful little timber town situated at the edge of a river and surrounded by tall trees and bush. A hotel, petrol station and a few shops were on the main street with houses scattered around them. After buying the few items I needed, I began my walk back to the house.

As I entered the lane I became aware of the dog again. It was as if he was waiting for me.

"Good dog," I ventured, not sure if I should be calling him. "Here, boy." But he cocked his head to one side and watched me. I walked on and he followed a few paces behind. When I reached the gate he disappeared into the bush. Should I coax him with food? He certainly didn't appear hungry so someone must be feeding him, but he wasn't wearing a collar.

I walked back into the house and decided it was time to get my laptop out and start work. For the rest of the afternoon I was lost in my novel, until I suddenly realised the light was fading outside. Stretching, I stood up and decided I needed coffee.

With a mug of coffee in my hand I wandered out the front door to watch the golden glow of the day merging into evening. And there he was again: my ghost dog, appearing and disappearing all the time.

He took a few steps towards me then turned back to the edge of the bush where he looked around at me again and sat down. It was almost like he wanted me to follow him, but with the night closing in I headed back inside. At the door I glanced back but he was gone.

The following day I decided to go for an early morning walk before working on my novel. It was cold and rain was threatening so I layered up in jumpers and jacket and added a beanie, scarf and heavy boots. I walked through the back gate and along the path leading through the bush. Not far along I saw Ghost Dog again, his pale form a shadow under the trees.

"Hello," I greeted him, extending my hand. But he ignored me and trotted away — not very far though, for a few minutes later there he was again, just ahead. Very cautious, I thought. Maybe he had been abused and was wary of people.

Before I could go any further the heavens suddenly opened and the rain bucketed down. The path rapidly turned to mud and I was quickly soaked. And my new best friend was gone again.

Thoughts of walking were quickly abandoned as I raced back to the house. Dry clothes, hot tea and work were what I needed right now.

As dark descended at the end of the day, I gazed out the window to see the dog sitting at the front door. I opened it but he ran off to the edge of the bush where he sat waiting. He does want me to follow him, I thought. But not tonight. Tomorrow hopefully it won't be so wet.

After a good night's sleep I woke to brilliant sunshine streaming through the window. Hot tea and toast and I was ready for my walk. And Ghost Dog was waiting at the back gate for me. How does he know which way I am going? As I opened the gate he trotted along the path, keeping a short distance between us, looking around to see if I was following.

I squelched through the mud and tried to avoid water as it dripped from the overhead branches, while my dog kept up a brisk pace ahead. We walked until the path disappeared into the undergrowth, but the dog trotted on. I stopped, wondering if I should go back. The bush looked very thick and I was sure I would soon be lost. However, Ghost Dog sat watching me, waiting, before turning back into the trees, so I decided to keep going. Going where? What on earth was this creature up to?

Just when I made up my mind to stop, the dog suddenly began to howl. This was the first time I had heard a sound from him and it was chilling. I felt the hairs stand up on my arms. As he stopped howling, he crouched down and put his head on his paws, staring intently at the ground. I stepped forward but he didn't move. I edged slowly closer and still he didn't move.

I was almost close enough to touch him when I saw what he was staring at. A hand was protruding from the ground. I stifled a scream and crept forward. He backed away and sat a little distance from me, watching. The ground around the hand was muddy and full of puddles, but I was able to see it was a human hand.

I grabbed my phone from my pocket and quickly rang the police, then sat shaking on a nearby log to wait. My companion sat quietly nearby, his tail slowly wagging.

When I heard the police coming, I looked at the dog. "You're a good dog," I said. "I wish I knew who you belong to." He looked back at me then stood up and trotted off into the trees. "Wait," I shouted. "Come back." But he was gone.

I explained to the police how I came to see the hand and a police-woman then walked me back to the house where I sat in a chair with a cup of tea and tried to figure out what was happening.

And I am still trying to figure it out. The hand belonged to a man who was buried with his wife and baby. They were the missing tenants of my house and they had been murdered and buried along with their clothes and possessions. Buried with them was their pet Samoyed dog.

The Cottage

The little stone cottage was gorgeous. It stood in the middle of lush green lawn, garden beds filled with geraniums, roses and lavender, and was surrounded by thick bush. We could hear the thunder of waves pounding the steep walls of the cliffs in the distance.

We had turned off the main road, followed the winding gravel track through the bush until it came to a sudden end, and there it was – built over a hundred years ago by a pioneering family of the district, and now open for tourists. After picking up a leaflet, strangely the only one at the tourist centre in town, we couldn't wait to have a look. And it just happened to be on the way to a beachside restaurant where we planned to have lunch.

At the gate a young man in wellington boots, his arms full of wood, grinned at us. "Hi there, you here to have a look around?"

"Yes, is it okay?" I nodded.

"Sure, follow me. I'm just getting wood for the fire."

We followed him across the damp lawn and onto the tiny front veranda. "This place is gorgeous," I said as we entered the front room. "I love it."

"Yeah, most people do." He handed us a brochure as we paid the entrance fee. "That'll give you a potted history of the cottage and grounds. We've only been open a few weeks. Feel free to wander." He smiled and turned to the fireplace. "I've almost let the fire go out and it's so bloody cold today."

"You can say that again," David agreed. "But winter's the best time to come. No crowds."

"Yeah, well, we wouldn't mind a few here. You from the city?"

"Yes, but we come here every year for a break. Check out the wineries, new places to eat and work on some new music."

"Music?"

"Yeah, we sing and I play keyboard. When we come down here the creative juices always flow, and we like it when it's cold with open fires everywhere."

"Yeah, when you don't forget to put on the wood. Cool about your music though."

"Right. Well, we'll go off for a look. See you in a while," David said.

We left him tending the fire to wander around. The room we were in was the sitting room, with furniture of the era scattered around – two wing chairs and an over-stuffed couch, a dresser displaying old vases and ornaments, and walls covered with photographs of people in hats and long dresses, all sternly staring at the camera. What a solemn lot they were.

A doorway to the right led to a bedroom with a very high four-poster brass bed complete with stepping stools. At each side of the bed were little tables with lamps and candles and in the corner stood a marble-topped stand with a large pitcher and bowl. Two white towels hung neatly over the rail in the front. More photos adorned the walls, with a lace curtain hanging at the window and a colourful rag rug covering the floorboards.

"Oh, this is so lovely," I whispered. "Just lovely. I feel as if I belong here."

"Strange, I sort of have that feeling too. But you'd swear someone is still living here."

"Mmm, I wish it was me."

We retraced our steps into the first room and through another door which took us into the biggest room in the house – a combined kitchen and dining room. The wood stove was alight and steam poured from the spout of the big black kettle on top. "This is unreal," I gasped, feeling the hairs on my arms standing on end. "Does someone really live here?"

"No."

At the sound of the voice, I jumped. But it was the young man, smiling at us. "I look after the place, collect the money, and do the gardening, so it seems a pity to waste a good fire. Besides, there's no electricity. My Mum comes down here sometimes and even makes scones for me. It's a great old stove. Name's Joe, by the way."

"Oh. I'm Claire, and this is my husband David."

"Nice to meet you. I'm just off out the back to do a bit of pruning. See you later."

I turned back to my explorations of the room. An assortment of pots and pans were displayed on a shelf above a cupboard and a table covered with a lace cloth was set for a meal with assorted china, cutlery and candles. Four wooden chairs were tucked in around the table.

We walked through the open back door to a small veranda and breathed in the heady scents of the garden which mingled with the damp bush and the salt of the ocean.

"This is just so good," I said, "I can't believe how nice it is."

"Certainly is. And look at the garden." David glanced around appreciatively. "So well kept."

One end of the veranda had been closed in, but the door was open. Inside was a beautiful white claw foot bath with a large towel draped over its side. A small table stood next to it with a collection of old bottles, jars and candles displayed on top. A larger table with a pitcher and bowl was in the corner. There was also a copper, with a fire set to burn.

"Oh, this is just too much. Look at that bath. Wouldn't it be wonderful to actually have a bath in it?" I looked at David.

"Yeah, now that would be an experience," he answered with a sly smile.

We wandered outside again and followed a path which led to a little wooden bridge spanning a stream. We stopped and looked across to the other side, where the path continued.

"Goes to the cliffs. Just a few minutes' walk if you have the time," Joe's voice called from across the lawn.

"Yes, we have the time," I smiled. Lunch could wait. Within five minutes, the bush cleared and we stood at the cliff top. The wind whipped at our clothes and spray from the waves below blew into our faces. "Wow, we'll be over the edge if we're not careful." I clutched at David and we carefully backed away. "I bet there are a few shipwrecks down there."

"Yeah, look at those rocks." He pointed and I could see the outline of jagged rocks close to the shoreline.

When we returned to the cottage, Joe was making himself a cup of tea. "What do you think? Really gets to you, doesn't it?"

"Sure does. We love it," David said.

"Well, I probably shouldn't tell you this right now, but the owners are thinking of letting people stay here for short breaks."

"Really?" Absolute seclusion. The perfect place to de-stress, write some new music. And in the middle of wonderful wine country. I could just picture it.

"There would be a few rules though. No pets or kids. And you would be living almost like the family who built this place – no electricity. No mod cons."

"How romantic. All those candles and open fires. And that gorgeous bath," I laughed.

"Yeah, but the hot water will have to come from the copper. The present owners have just added on that bathroom. I think the first family would probably have used an old tin tub for their baths."

"Well, we're certainly interested." David said. "What if we give you our phone numbers and you can let us know what the owners decide?"

"Sure. No problem."

Later, as we sat in a cafe enjoying a delightful lunch, we couldn't stop talking about the cottage.

"I feel I could write some really good music there, honey."

"Me too. There's something about that place … I can't quite put my finger on it …"

"I know just what you mean. I feel it's pulling at me. Isn't that strange?" I put my hand on David's arm. "We must have it, sweetheart, we must."

"Yes, I agree. What if we call in on the way back to our cabin and have another chat with Joe?"

"Absolutely."

A few weeks later our biggest gig, at a five-star restaurant, was cancelled due to a kitchen fire. They were going to be out of action for three weeks. Two other gigs in that time were also cancelled due to double-booking. Very unusual. Then we had a phone call from Jane Lewis who owned the cottage with her husband, Grant. Were we interested in renting the cottage for a week as a trial run? Were we ever!

"This was meant to be, you know that don't you?" I said to David.

"I kind of had that idea too. So, are we ready for another chill-out then?"

"You bet. Fancy getting away twice in two months. I can't believe it."

We could barely see the road let alone the cottage. The rain was sheeting down when we arrived in the afternoon. The gate had been left open so we parked as close to the front veranda as we could then made a dash for the door. We had picked up the keys from the tourist centre in town and bought milk and two lovely T-bone steaks from the butcher, as well as a wonderful sourdough loaf from the bakery, adding to the supplies we brought from home.

We stood shivering in the doorway as David turned the key, but as soon as we stepped inside we were overtaken by a warm, relaxing feeling. A fire was crackling in the grate and oil lamps were shedding their cosy glow around the room. Joe appeared from the kitchen.

"Hello again," he grinned. "Hope you're not too wet."

"Oh, we'll soon dry off," I laughed, holding my hands out to the fire. "Did you do all this?"

"Yeah, part of the deal. Fires are going in the bedroom and kitchen, and the copper is alight too, otherwise you'll have no hot water for baths. Well, I'll be off. There's a note from Jane in the kitchen, with phone numbers if you need to contact us. I suppose you have your mobiles?"

"Of course. We'd rather leave them home, but in our business that's not a good idea. Thanks, Joe," David said, taking off his jacket.

"Okey doke. There's also a little kero fridge with milk in case you haven't brought any with you. See you later then."

When we went through to the kitchen there was another nice surprise. The kettle was bubbling away on the hob, and under a tea towel on the table was a wonderful plate of warm scones. Oh I was going to love this week. After changing into dry clothes we made coffee, buttered the scones and sat in the sitting room in front of the fire.

"I think I'll just curl up here and not move for days," I murmured, tucking my legs under me. "This is bliss."

"Yeah, what a way to spend an afternoon. I think I will too." David smiled and stretched out his long legs. "There's something about fires on a wet day."

"Mmm, yes. Romantic," I sighed, looking at the rug in front of the fire.

He followed my gaze and a slow smile spread over his handsome face. "Yes, very romantic."

After a candlelit dinner of steak and salad we sat in front of the fire with a glass of red and Frank Sinatra on our portable CD player. Outside, thunder rumbled across the black sky and lightning flashed at the windows. At least we didn't have to worry about power failures.

"I think I'll go to bed," I murmured finally. After travelling from the city and enjoying a nice meal, not to mention the wine, my eyes were suddenly very heavy.

"Yeah, me too. The fire's almost out. I think I must have dozed off."

"Yes, you did. Just put the screen in front and I'll put out the lamps."

We sank into our lovely comfortable bed and, with the lights out, were enveloped by complete blackness. "It's a bit scary, isn't it?" I whispered. "We're so used to street lights outside."

"Mmm."

I don't know how long I had been asleep, but suddenly I was wide awake. It was eerily quiet, no wind or rain. Just silence. But something had woken me. I listened, but nothing. Then as I drifted off again I heard a soft sound, a muffled baby's cry. It seemed so close. I pulled the covers around me. Don't be stupid, I told myself. You're just imagining things.

Next morning the storm had passed and the day was cool and crisp with a weak sun shining. David got the fires going and the rooms soon warmed. We made a lovely breakfast of thick toast, over the flames of course, slathered with butter and chunky homemade marmalade, which we found in the pantry. And strong tea in perfect china cups.

Then something caught my eye. "Honey, look. That book wasn't there last night." I pointed to a leather-bound book on top of the fridge.

"You sure? 'course it was. You just didn't notice."

"No, it wasn't there." I picked it up and flicked through yellowed pages. "It's old. Seems to be a family history of this place, but with no author's name. I wonder where it came from."

"It was probably here all the time, you just didn't see it."

"No, I know it wasn't, but I'll certainly enjoy reading it. This house fascinates me."

"Okay, so what are we going to do today then? Go out or stay in and be creative? Or are you going to read that?" David smiled.

"Oh, I think I'd like to go for a walk, then maybe lunch somewhere. We can be creative this afternoon."

"Good idea. Just as well we thought to bring our wellies, it looks pretty damp out there."

"Yeah, let's go now. Dishes can wait."

We spent a delightful morning discovering little trails into the bush, most of which ended at the cliff top, then had a lovely lunch at a little cafe overlooking a vineyard. In the afternoon, we opened a bottle of chardonnay and a jar of olives and sat down to some serious writing.

David tuned his guitar while I set up my keyboard in the corner of the lounge. A shiver went through me as I did so and for a moment I felt very cold. As the afternoon turned into evening, we decided to have dinner at a winery not far away. The night was cold but there was a clear starry sky, so we opted to walk. Rugged up in our jackets and scarves, we set off for a great meal in front of a huge log fire.

"I hope our fire is still going," I said, rubbing my hands together as we returned to the cottage."

"Yep, still going," David declared as he removed the screen. "I'll just stoke it a bit. What's wrong?" He was looking at me. I was standing in the middle of the room staring at my keyboard.

"I'm sure I stacked that music up," I said slowly, looking at the pile of scattered music sheets on the floor.

"I bet it was a draft."

"Maybe, but there hasn't been any wind tonight. Never mind, I'll pick it up and stack it again."

"Feel like a coffee? I can put the kettle on here."

"Yeah, why not. But definitely nothing to eat. I'm not going to eat for a week after that meal."

"Yes, wasn't it good? But don't forget that Devonshire tea tomorrow …"

"Don't remind me, the thought makes me feel sick. I'm just going to sit here and enjoy my coffee while I read that book."

William and Alice Cooper built the cottage after they arrived from England with their two sons and daughter in 1880, and it had stayed in the family until recently when the last relative had died. No other relations had been located so it was bought by Jane and Grant Lewis, and they had done a wonderful job with the restoration.

As I lost myself in the book, David dozed and the fire gradually burned down. It had grown windy outside and every now and then it gusted down the chimney or rattled the windows, making the lamps flicker. I stretched and put the book down. It was just so interesting. After the family moved into the cottage, two more daughters were born. William began a successful timber business, the two eldest children, Albert and Charles, married and moved into the town, and their sister Ada stayed home to help her mother with her two little sisters.

I picked up the book again and read a few more pages. As I did so the wind suddenly howled around the house and a huge clap of thunder woke David. He stared at me for a minute then, realising where he was, smiled and closed his eyes.

"David," I whispered. "This is really weird. David …"

"What?" he muttered, sitting up.

"Just as I was reading about a violent storm happening, it really is happening."

"What do you mean?"

"Well, apparently there was a terrible storm here and I'm just up to the part where a ship has hit the rocks out there near the cliffs. And just listen to that storm outside now." As I spoke, the lightning flashed at the windows, illuminating the entire room, and rain leaked down the wall near the door. "It's scary out there." I shivered and moved closer to the fire.

"It's all right, hon. Don't worry. Hey, come over here." He patted the sofa where he sat. I moved next to him and he put his arm around me. "Just as well we're in here and not out there," he laughed.

"Yeah, right. But it's strange how I was reading about the storm, and it was really happening." A gust of wind blew down the chimney and the fire hissed as spits of rain hit the flames. Suddenly, the music sheets I had re-stacked floated to the floor.

"See, I told you it was a draft," David laughed. But I shivered again. I had gone very cold. "Claire, what's wrong?"

"I don't know. But I'm so cold and I can feel the hairs on my arms standing up. Can't you feel something?"

"No."

"I … I think there … there's something here." I stood up and walked to the music sheets which were fluttering on the floor. "Something weird is happening. I can feel it."

"Claire." In a stride, David was next to me, holding me in his arms. "You *are* cold. What is it, babe?"

"David, you must be able to feel it. There's a presence in this room, I just know it."

"Well, I know it's a bit drafty in here but I can't feel anything. Come and sit down and I'll make you a coffee." He sat me on the sofa and wrapped a throw rug around my shoulders.

Then, everything was normal once more. I stopped shivering

and leaned back. "It's gone. Whatever it was, it's gone. Oh, David, I think we have a ghost in here."

He looked at me and laughed. "A ghost? Well, the place is old, but …"

"I must read some more of the book. Maybe we can find out."

"Ok, I'll make the coffee." He disappeared into the kitchen and I picked up the book.

Apparently, when the storm had subsided, the family went down to the beach and found a young man lying on the sand. They brought him back to the cottage and nursed him back to health. His name was George Walker. As he recovered he stayed with them and fell in love with their daughter Ada. And he used to play her piano …

The hair on my arms promptly rose again as I heard music. I looked towards my keyboard. The keys were moving by themselves. "David! David!"

"What? Are you alright? I heard the …" He stood, frozen to the spot as he too saw the keys moving. Then, all was normal once more. It had only lasted a few seconds but felt like minutes. He was at my side, arms around me again. "What's going on?"

"I … I was reading … David, this is so strange. Before I was reading about the storm and there was one outside; this time I was reading about George Walker, who was washed up on the beach during the storm and found by the Coopers. They looked after him and he fell in love with Ada. And … and he played piano for her. As … as I read it … it happened. I'm almost too scared to read any more."

David walked over to the keyboard and peered closely at it then turned to me. "Read some more."

I stared at him and slowly opened the book. But the next few pages told only about George working for William in his timber business, and the death of their two youngest daughters.

"Let's go to bed. I've had enough for one night," David said finally, pulling me to my feet. "Tomorrow's another day." And I had to agree.

As the next day was fine we decided to check out some galleries and maybe even venture into the caves. We hadn't done that in years. By five in the afternoon we arrived home, tired but armed with a bag of gourmet goodies from a delightful shop in the town.

"Let's have a wine and go through some music, then I'll make dinner," I suggested, pulling off my jacket.

"Good idea." We settled down for the next two hours and made good progress. I even managed to write a song.

After dinner we relaxed with some music in front of the fire for a while, until David fell asleep. "C'mon, time for bed," I nudged him. "It's bucketing down again out there. We should be snuggled under the bed clothes."

We burrowed down into the lovely warmth of the bed and I picked up the book once more. David looked at me with a frown.

"It's alright," I assured him. "I'm okay."

The next few pages told more of the family history – babies, new arrivals from England, the death of an aunt, and the marriage of George to Ada. They lived with her parents while George built a cottage in the town. Then Ada fell pregnant.

A loud roll of thunder startled me and a lightning flash illuminated the room. Not another storm. I moved further down under the covers. But I had to keep reading. Ada had a baby girl named Lucy but they couldn't move into their new home because George was ill and hadn't finished the roof of their cottage.

Finally, it was ready, but then tragedy struck when Lucy became ill and died.

Why were they all getting sick and dying? I suddenly went cold. I felt so sick I thought I would vomit. What was happening to me? David slept on but I didn't wake him. I wanted to keep reading. Needed to.

Lucy had only been in her grave a week before George had to bury Ada. He was distraught. One day when …

I stopped reading. I could hear music. My keyboard.

I looked back at the page … when he was alone at home he pushed the piano out of the house and into the stream …

My blood ran cold as I heard loud thumps and the sound of furniture falling. I looked at David but strangely, he remained asleep. I tried to get out of bed but couldn't move. I could only lay there and listen to the noises. I heard the back door slam against the wall and the loud drumming of rain. Then a piercing scream rent the air, before silence descended. No rain. No storm. Nothing.

Then I could move again. I prodded David before I slowly got out of bed. What was I going to find? But I was determined. "David, wake up. Quick." He sat up, saw that I was out of bed.

"What's wrong, honey? Are you alright?"

"No, I'm not alright. Something's going on out there. I don't know how all that noise didn't wake you. Something was playing my keyboard, and then noises like furniture being pushed over. We've got to find out what's happening."

Entering the room was like entering a bad dream. Chairs were tipped over and things were strewn all over the floor. And my keyboard was missing. I raced to the kitchen where the back door was wide open and the floor was wet with rain. All was quiet outside.

"Bloody hell! What's been happening? How did I sleep through this?"

"Well, I don't think it's your fault really. Something kept you asleep, and wouldn't let me out of bed. I was literally frozen to the spot. Shall we look outside?"

"I'll get the torch, but it's so black out there, we should really wait until morning."

"No, we can't wait. David, it's that book. Everything I read starts happening to us. This is so weird."

"Claire, go and get it …"

"What? Before … we … we go outside you mean?"

"Yes. If what you say is true I think we should know what's going to happen before we go out there, don't you?"

Nodding my agreement, I ran back to the bedroom and grabbed the book. I found the pages I had been reading, and began to feel sick again. William and Alice returned to the cottage to find the piano half submerged in the stream and George hanging from a gum tree in the garden. David pushed me into a chair. "Stay there. I'm going to look outside."

"No, don't leave me here. I want to come with you." I hung onto his arm. "We'll go out there together."

Outside, the night was still, as if there had been no storm at all. But there, half submerged in the stream, was my keyboard and in a nearby tree a thick rope swung from a branch …

When I woke I found myself back in bed. David was stroking my forehead and had a frown on his own. "How are you feeling, love? You fainted," he said.

"I'm okay. What's happening?" I sat up.

"Nothing. Everything seems normal again. Well, almost normal, but you'll have to wait until morning for me to retrieve your keyboard. Then I think we should get the hell out of here."

"Yes, but David, I've got to read the rest of the book. I have to know what happened."

"I knew you'd say that. In the meantime I've stoked the fire and put the kettle on to make some tea. Then we're both going to get some sleep, if that's possible. Tomorrow we'll sort everything out. Im just wondering why we weren't told this place was bloody haunted."

"Well that's obvious. Would we still have come?"

"Definitely not! Now relax while I do the tea."

Then I remembered why I had fainted. "David … the rope …"

"Ah …well, yeah, that's still there. Buggered if I know where it came from."

I sat up. "David, give me the book."

"Not now, Claire. Later. You need to rest."

"No I don't. Please, David …"

"Okay, here you are, but don't get out of bed. Just stay there and I'll be back."

I quickly found the page I had been reading – where the family returned home and discovered George hanging from the tree. He was buried with his wife and baby. Tears stung my eyes. The poor man. He must have loved her so much to want to follow her to the grave. How horrible all this was.

David came in with the tea – nice and strong and hot. "So, what happened next?"

"George was buried with his wife and baby. It's all so sad …"

"Yes, it is but we're leaving first thing in the morning. I'll give Jane and Grant a call and let them know what's been happening here."

"Absolutely! I can't stay here another day, it's too frightening."

When we finished the tea, David returned to the kitchen with the cups while I read some more. A year after the tragedy, Alice died. William found her body on the rocks at the bottom of the cliffs after a wild storm.

"David," I called. "This family history is unbelievable."

"This whole thing is unbelievable," he said as he came into the room and climbed into bed. "What now?"

"Well, first George is sick but doesn't die, then baby Lucy is sick and she dies, followed by Ada. And don't forget Ada's two little sisters. What do you think made them die?"

"God I don't know. Maybe there was a sickness that was contagious, or maybe they ate something poisonous. You know how it was back then."

"Mmm, bit funny though, don't you think. Then George goes mad and hangs himself. Then Alice dies a year later. What would she have been doing out there on a stormy night to fall off the edge of the cliffs?"

"Well, maybe she was scared and running away or something."

"Scared? Of what?"

"George's ghost? God, I don't know, Claire. This is ridiculous."

"No it's not. Maybe George was haunting the place way back then. But what about William and the other two kids? Let's see …" I picked up the book again. "William stayed here alone. After he died one of his grandchildren came to live here. Flora. She lived alone apparently, never married, and stayed here with her cat and … a … piano. Oh my God, I wonder what happened to her."

"I can guess. Her piano finished up in the stream?"

"Um … oh no! Some of the family came to visit her after a particularly bad storm and found the piano … in … in the stream. Flora was nowhere to be found, but later she was discovered … on the rocks where Alice had died. Oh this is just horrible. What awful things have gone on in this house?"

"Well, it seems that no one can bring a keyboard here without upsetting George. There are lots of storms. Lots of deaths …"

"Well, something must have started this chain of events. Why were they all sick? Do you think someone was trying to kill them?"

"Oh, Claire, who would do that?"

"I don't know. Alice maybe?"

"Alice! She wouldn't kill her family … kill a baby. Surely."

"What if she was mad? What if she didn't like girls? All the kids who died were girls."

"Possibly. But what about Ada? Read some more."

"After Flora's death the family decided to leave the house. No-one wanted to live in it. Then John Cooper came from England and moved in. There's an excerpt here from one of his letters: 'My Great Aunt Alice's madness does not worry me, nor does the tragedy of family deaths. I do not believe she killed the girls nor do I believe George can harm me, or that anyone who lives in this house will die. I will live here with my piano and prove this is a foolishness.' My God, David, Alice *was* mad. She must have killed poor little Lucy and Ada and probably her two little daughters too, and maybe tried to kill George but failed. Now he's taken over the house, and … oh God, we're staying here!"

"Mmm, but we're not *living* here. What next?"

"Ah, another storm. Oh!" I stopped as the wind whipped up outside and the rain lashed the window. "No, not again."

"It's okay, Claire honey. Don't worry. Put the book away."

"No! I want to see what happens to John. 'Lightning struck a tree'… what was that?"

An enormous crash sounded as lightning flashed at the windows.

"Sounds like … a tree being struck!"

"Oh no. David, it says here that John … John's body was found at the bottom of … of the cliffs and his piano in the stream. Oh this is horrible."

"Bloody horrible! Surely you must be at the end of the book by now, Claire."

"Well, yes, I think so … David! Look! The rest of the book … the pages are all blank!"

"That's it. We're leaving. Now! C'mon, Claire. Get up."

But then I saw it and screamed. "Ssss … someone's in the doorway." A young man with shaggy dark hair. Floating towards us. Somewhere a baby cried and a woman screamed. David grabbed me and we ran to the door. But the figure floated behind us.

"Run, Claire. Quick!" David pulled at the front door but it wouldn't open. "The back door. Quick."

As we turned I screamed again. The figure hovered over me. Panicking, I clung to David as he almost dragged me from the room.

When we reached the kitchen the door flew open and we felt ourselves sucked into the fury of the storm. We clutched at the door, trying to keep our feet, but the wind pulled more furiously at us until we were blown along the path towards the stream. Past the half submerged keyboard and over the bridge; onwards towards the cliff top. Our feet were barely touching the ground as we grabbed in vain at passing tree branches. David clutched my hand tightly as we tried to gain a foothold near the edge, where we hovered precariously … … …

The storm was gone and the night was clear and calm. The book lay on the bed in the cottage, its pages fluttering open as if by a breeze. The story of Claire and David filled the blank pages.

Jack

It all started when I found the photo lying on the grass in my local park. The face of a handsome soldier stared up at me, his dark eyes connecting with mine.

On the back of the photo the words *Gallipoli 1915* were written in faded ink. But no name. I turned the photo over and gazed at that lovely face again. He looked so young – too young to be a soldier. I carefully put it in my bag, but for the rest of the day I couldn't stop thinking about him. Who was he? Did he have a family?

For the next week that young boy stayed on my mind, and I wondered if it was a coincidence when, reading the travel pages in *The West Australian*, I saw an ad for a trip to Turkey, including Gallipoli.

On impulse, I phoned the agency and made a booking for the following month. I'd never done anything like that before – most of my trips were well planned. But at least I had holidays due at work.

"Well, Jack," I said, looking at the photo which was now propped up on my bedside table, "I'm off to Gallipoli and I don't really know why. How does that work?"

For some reason I had named him Jack and as he looked at me from under his slouch hat, I thought I saw him smile. Was I going mad?

I had a smooth flight to Istanbul and was soon checked into my hotel room with its view across the Bosphorus. With growing excitement I put Jack next to my bed. Was that another smile?

The next day our group set off on a walk through the city, stopping to enjoy Turkish coffee and pastries at a little café before visits to the Blue Mosque and Topkapi Museum, so beautiful and full of history. I found myself falling in love with the city and all its historic buildings.

After another day of tours through the Hagia Sophia and the maze of laneways inside the Grand Bazaar, I was eager for my trip to Gallipoli.

The next afternoon we crossed the Dardanelles on a massive ferry to Canakkale and I could hardly contain the feelings growing inside me. Why was I reacting this way to a photograph of someone I didn't know? If I had to explain it to anyone they would definitely think I was mad, but the fact was that face in the photo had me mesmerised – almost as if I had been hypnotised. It was driving me on to … … to what? I didn't know.

It was very emotional for all of us when we arrived at Anzac Cove, trying to imagine what it was like for all those unfortunate men, who, when they landed, were confronted with those towering cliffs.

I had Jack close to me in my pocket as I walked among the graves, finally finding myself in front of the Lone Pine Memorial. I reached out to touch the panels which named over 3,000 missing Australian soldiers, and as I did so I was overcome with dizziness and couldn't believe I was about to faint.

I was woken by unbelievably loud noises. I covered my ears and looked around. *Gun fire!* And I was lying in a trench. A trench filled with bodies.

Surely I was dreaming. This could not possibly be true. I staggered to my feet and leaned on the earth wall as soldiers ran past, seemingly oblivious to my presence.

Suddenly someone touched my arm and I looked into that handsome young face. *Jack.*

"Sit down," he said, as if it was perfectly normal for me to be in a trench filled with dead and dying men a hundred years ago.

Numbly I sat down and he slid down beside me. "Tell me this isn't true," I whispered. "I'm dreaming, aren't I?"

"No, Stella, you're not."

"How do you know my name?"

"I brought you here. I don't know how, but when you found my photo we connected. I want you to see how I died. I want you to tell my family."

"But … but I don't know your family … and … and if I've gone back in time, how will I get home again?"

"I don't know how this works either, but I'm sure you will find your way."

"What's your name?"

"Jack. Jack Kennedy."

"Really? It's really Jack?"

"Yes. I told you — we have a connection, though I'm not sure how."

"I think we do too. I've felt drawn to you since I found your photo, and I don't understand why either. I've never thought of visiting Turkey, let alone Gallipoli, yet here I am. And here I am, a hundred years in the past. How?"

"I don't know but I know you're here because of me. I needed you to find me, to know what happened to me."

"Why can't these men see me like you can?" I nodded towards them, all running past. "They can't see you either, can they?"

"No. I'm already dead."

"Oh God! I don't believe this. Tell me what happened. You look so young – too young to die."

"I'm eighteen and we're all too young to die. Just look around you, all those bodies we have to walk over – some are even Turks. We have burial parties getting the bodies out of the way, but more just take their place. They keep piling up. We eat, drink and try to sleep amongst our dead – it's bloody awful! Trying not to walk on them, feeling them soft under our boots when we do. You can't avoid the blood, the stench …" His voice broke and he bent his head. "I can't imagine a worse horror. Smoking and talking about our families and sweethearts keeps us going."

"Do you have a sweetheart?"

"Yes. Her name is Ivy. The most wonderful person with such lovely red hair. We were going to be married after the war. She doesn't know I'm dead. They'll never find me …"

"What happened?"

"It was my turn to go over the top. I was at the front and don't remember anything. At least it was quick, but there are pieces of me everywhere out there." His voice faltered. "Here's her address. Or at least it was all those years ago." He handed me a photo of a beautiful smiling woman with the inscription 'To my darling Jack, from your girl, Ivy. I will wait for you.' He had written her address on the back.

"Oh, Jack." I reached out to touch him but as I did he faded slowly away. The tears rolled down my cheeks as I looked at the photo. Her beauty was so out of place amid the bodies, the smell and the gunfire.

I stood up and looked at the desolation around me, at all those men who would soon be dead. It was hard to believe that one day the Lone Pine Cemetery would be on this very spot. And now I had to somehow find my way back. But as I thought about it the dizziness returned and I felt myself falling …

"Are you okay?" The voice sounded a thousand miles away. I opened my eyes and saw the face of one of our group bending over me. "Stella, you fainted. Let me help you up." Her arms went around me and she helped me to my feet.

"I'm okay, I think," I said. "How long have I been out to it?"

"About five minutes. Not long."

Only a hundred years long. "Thanks Betty, I'm okay now." I rummaged in my bag which was lying at my feet and found my water bottle. "Well, I'd better finish looking around before it's time to be back on the coach," I smiled at her questioning face. "I feel fine. Honestly."

"All right. But let me know if I can do anything."

"Thanks, I will."

As I walked away I put my hand in my pocket. "Jack," I murmured, and when I pulled out his photo another one fluttered to the ground. I stared in disbelief at the photo of Ivy.

Whichever way I looked at what happened there was no explanation. My trip back in time was so real – the smells, the sounds, even Jack – and I had Ivy's photo to prove it all.

Back home in Perth, I decided to check out the address Jack had given me. It was a suburb near my house. Another coincidence?

The house was old and run-down. In answer to my knock, an elderly woman opened the door a little way and peered out.

"Yes?" she asked.

"I don't know if I have the right address, but I was wondering if a woman named Ivy ever lived here." I showed her the photo as I spoke.

"Ivy? Why yes, yes she did. A long time ago."

"Can I come in? I would like to talk to you about her." I really didn't know how I was going to explain the photo. "My name is Stella."

"Yes, come in. I'm Elizabeth Miller. Ivy was my grandmother."

"Grandmother! How lovely. I can't believe this has been so easy. I thought I would have a much longer search."

"Please sit down. Would you like some tea?"

"Yes, that would be nice. Then I'll try to tell my story without you thinking I'm crazy."

When the tea was ready I showed Elizabeth the photo of Jack. "He was going to marry Ivy but unfortunately he died in Gallipoli."

"How did you know that? He's actually my grandfather."

"Really? How … … oh, I see."

"Yes, Ivy was pregnant but unfortunately they weren't married so she lived here with her parents and had Matilda, my mother. Ivy never married and I've lived here since my husband died. We have a daughter, Jane. But how do you know about Jack?"

"Well," I took a deep breath and began my story, sure that Elizabeth would certainly want me to leave. When I finished I picked up my cup and drank my tea, waiting for a response.

"It's funny but I do believe you. Otherwise how could you possibly know all this, and have the photos too?"

"Thank you Elizabeth."

At that moment there was a knock on the door.

"That will be my grandson, Toby. I was expecting him. I won't be a moment."

Elizabeth left the room and returned with a tall, dark haired man who smiled at me.

"Hi, I'm Toby," he said. I sat, stunned. Toby was an older version of Jack. He extended his hand, and as I took it a shock rippled through me. What was happening to me now?

During the following months Toby and I spent a lot of time together. We had so much in common. Besides music and history, neither of us had ever married or had serious relationships. He never doubted my story of Gallipoli, thankfully believing I wasn't crazy, and a year later we were married.

After a blissful honeymoon in Turkey we found we were expecting a baby. Our son, Jack.

The Last Protest

The house was cold, but Joan didn't care. She sat on the bed, pulled her bedspread around her shoulders and wriggled her toes inside her fluffy slippers.

It was years since Harry had rubbed her feet. She always had cold feet in winter but he used to massage them with his warm hands. He had done so many things for her. Funny how you didn't think about it until it was too late. He was gone now, at least physically, but the memories remained.

This old house was full of memories. Sixty years ago Harry had built it and then carried his young bride over the threshold.

His spirit was everywhere, lingering like morning mists. She saw him in his favourite chair near the fire, smiling at her over his paper. She saw him in the garden, bending over his rose bushes. Of course he was still here – how could they say otherwise.

And the sounds – they echoed around the house – she could hear them. Babies crying, children laughing, dogs barking. The house wasn't really empty at all. Couldn't they understand that?

Joan stood up, looked down at Ernie. His big brown eyes stared hopefully at her as his tail thumped the floor.

"No, not today, my love," she said softly to him. "It's too cold outside for me. Maybe tomorrow." She bent slowly and fondled his ears. "Sorry, boy."

Trying to keep the bedspread wrapped around her, Joan turned on the television and returned to her bed. Making herself comfortable, she focused on the programme. But, inevitably, her mind wandered. Why couldn't she concentrate these days? It seemed her thoughts were always going back to when Harry was alive, and the children were all at home.

Time couldn't stand still, no matter how much you wanted it to. The past would stay in the corridors of her mind. She couldn't bring it back. Why didn't happy times last? Why did they fade like old clothes, only to be talked about at family gatherings? Remember when …

But times were different now. When Harry died everyone said she would be lonely, but she wasn't. Of course, he wasn't there to rub her feet or hold her close when she needed comfort, but she could still talk to him. She could feel his presence in every room.

Everyone said the house would be too big, but it wasn't. It was a lovely friendly place and she had never felt scared or threatened. Until now.

Her thoughts were interrupted by an urgent knocking. Ernie was barking and she hadn't even heard him. Opening the door a little, she peered out to see who her visitor was.

"Hello, Joan." Mark Watson was standing there, a worried frown on his face. "Are you alright?"

"Of course. Why shouldn't I be?"

"Well, I've been knocking for ages and I could hear Ernie barking. I thought, maybe …"

"Don't be silly! I'm fine. What do you want?"

"Can I come in for a minute? I have to talk to you."

"I suppose so." Joan stepped back, allowing Mark to enter the dim hallway. "What do you want?" she said again.

"Joan … I …"

"I don't want to talk about it."

"Please, Joan." He gripped her shoulders gently. "You must listen to me."

"No!"

"Joan! You've got to face it. I've been patient with you these past five weeks, but your time has run out. There's nothing you can do any more."

"I'm not moving!"

"Look, Joan, you've got no choice. I gave you two weeks' rent here after the sale of this place – your family told me that was all the time you would need. You've had five weeks and I can't give you any more. Do you hear me, Joan? There is no more time!"

"But … my unit isn't ready …"

"Your unit *is* ready, and you know it is. All your things are there. Look around you – there's almost nothing left here. *And* it's freezing! You don't have to live like this when you have a comfortable unit not ten minutes from here."

Joan looked solemnly around the room, not wanting to see its bleakness. Her heart suddenly felt heavy, and, as if understanding her thoughts, Ernie nuzzled her legs and flopped onto her feet.

"Come on, Joan. All you've got here are your TV and your bed. You can't expect your family to keep bringing your meals. Don't you understand?"

"Yes, I understand." The words came slowly as she sank onto the bed, the bedspread slipping from her sagging shoulders.

She couldn't shut it out any more. In despair, she had to face it. She had to face the future. It was there and it wouldn't go away.

"Alright," she whispered. "Alright."

"Can I phone your family and tell them you're ready now?"

"Yes."

"Promise?"

"Yes. I promise." Joan looked up at him with tear-filled eyes. "Yes!"

"Good. I'm glad you've finally seen reason. I'll give them a call. Will you be okay for a few minutes?"

"Of course. I live here!"

As she heard the door close, the tears rolled down her cheeks. I'm sorry, Harry, I'm sorry. I have to go. I have to leave. Please understand.

"Hello Mum," a cheery voice called. "I've come to take you home. Are you ready?" Barbara came eagerly into the room. "Oh, it's so cold in here. You must be freezing."

"No, I'm alright."

"Ready then? C'mon, Ernie, wait till you see your new home." She put a firm arm around her mother, guiding her to the front door, afraid that she might change her mind again.

"My TV … my bed …"

"Don't worry; Bob's coming after work with the trailer."

They stepped onto the front porch and Joan blinked at the brightness of the day.

"C'mon, Mum, into the car before you catch cold." Barbara's voice was urgent, but her mother remained motionless.

As if poised for battle, a row of huge machines stood facing her, silently waiting for a signal to roar into life.

Joan looked up and down the street. But it was quiet and deserted. She was surrounded by mounds of rubble and piles of sand. She was the last one – the last to make a personal protest at progress. But she had lost and the future had won. Her past would soon be gone forever.

The Crimson Cloak

The scream came from outside the house and had everyone running. Margaret's body lay shattered, her eyes wide and staring, her blood a crimson cloak around her.

"Oh my God! Margaret!" Andrea Martin reached her first.

"What happened?" Greg was close behind. "Oh God! Dear God!" He bent over the girl.

"She's fallen from her window," Andrea sobbed, looking up at the open window of Margaret's upstairs bedroom. She looked back at the still body of their daughter with disbelief and shook her head.

"Is she dead?" The question came from Joel, standing near the front door.

"Oh my beautiful Margaret, my beautiful girl. Please don't die!"

Joel didn't move. "You always said she shouldn't sit there in case she fell."

The sun shone from a bright blue sky as Joel brought in the mail. "Only one today," he smiled at Emma as he tossed the letter on the table.

"Who is it for?" she asked, turning from the sink where she stood washing dishes.

"Me, but I'll read it later. It's probably a bill and I'll be late for work if I don't leave now." Joel kissed her and walked to the door. "See you tonight." Emma looked at the letter and sighed. He could have taken it with him. She propped it on the sideboard and returned to her dishes.

"Don't forget to read your letter, it might be important," Emma nodded towards the sideboard as they sat down to dinner.

"Oh, yeah, okay," Joel picked it up and tore it open. "Hmm, I wonder who it's from."

"Are you okay? Is it bad news?" Emma leaned forward, touched his hand. "You've gone pale."

"It's from a lawyer. My father has died and I am needed to finalise things."

"Oh I'm so sorry."

"Don't be. I'm not."

"Joel! Don't say that. He was your father."

"Maybe, but I haven't seen him for forty years or been home in that time. They didn't care."

"That's all you've ever told me, and apart from your mother dying a few years ago, I don't really know much about your family at all, Joel."

"You know all you need to know. We've had ten good years together. We're happy and we don't need anyone else."

"Just because I don't have a family doesn't mean you can't tell me about yours. At least you weren't brought up in an orphanage like me." Emma gripped his hand. "Please tell me something at least, if we have to go to your home."

Joel pulled away from her and pushed his chair back angrily. "What makes you think you'll be coming with me?"

"For support … you know I'll always support you. Why won't you tell me?"

"You want to know? You want to know do you?" he shouted suddenly. "Well I came from a family where everything revolved around my sister …"

"A sister? But that's really good, we can contact her and …"

"She's dead!"

"Oh. I'm sorry."

"Sorry again? I'm not. She was five years older than me and never liked me, always bossing me around, pinching me if I didn't do what she wanted. My parents always believed her, she could twist anyone around her finger. Margaret was stunningly beautiful and very intelligent while I was just ordinary."

"Oh Joel." Emma stood up; put her arms around him. "You're not ordinary. How did she die?"

"She fell out of her bedroom window when she was fifteen."

"How dreadful! Your poor parents!"

"Yeah, poor parents. For the next five years I was even more ordinary. They never got over losing their precious daughter and practically ignored me, so I left school when I was fifteen and ran away. I've never been back and they never even tried to find me. So now you know more about me. Satisfied?"

"Yes. Look at me, Joel," Emma turned his face to hers. "I love you and I'll always support you. Let me come with you so you can put an end to everything. Forget your past and think of our future."

"Wow! It's such a big house," Emma said as they stood at the gate. "Are you sure you want to sell it?"

"What do you think? I don't even want to go inside, let alone live in it. As soon as we've sorted everything I'll put it on the market and we can leave."

"Okay, but it might take a few days, judging by the size of the place. Are you alright with that?"

"I'll have to be."

Joel unlocked the front door and they walked into the dark interior of the large entry hall. "There are a lot of rooms but I think we'll start upstairs in the study. We can probably sleep in my old room." He turned on the lights and led the way up the stairs and along a passage, stopping in front of a closed door. "In there."

Emma opened the door and switched on the light. The room was huge and was as Joel had left it at fifteen. He looked around, shaking his head at the unmade bed and clothes on the floor. "Bloody hell! Looks like after I left they just shut the door and forgot about me."

"If you want to sleep in another room …"

"No, this will do, we can clean it up a bit. I'll show you the rest of the house so we can get started. I just want to sort out the documents and get the secondhand shop to pick up everything else. I don't want anything."

"Alright, whatever you like." Emma hugged him. "Everything will be okay."

Joel spent the rest of the day sorting the documents he found in the study into boxes while Emma cleaned the kitchen and investigated the pantry to make dinner.

"I can do a pasta tonight but I'll need a few things tomorrow," she said as they sat at the dining room table.

"Okay but a couple of days only, we'll be gone after that."

"I'll go first thing in the morning so I can be back to help you. Joel, how does it feel to be back here after forty years?"

"Awful! This place hasn't changed, it's just as I remembered it. And I still hate it."

"Oh well, at least your parents didn't write you out of the will."

"Yeah, that was a surprise, but I don't understand why."

When Joel woke the next morning he found Emma's note on the pillow next to him. *"Gone into town. Be back soon. Love Em xx"*. He couldn't believe he hadn't heard her leave. Dressing quickly, he made his way downstairs to the kitchen and filled the kettle. As he turned to the stove he glanced into the living room and froze.

In the middle of the room a woman lay on her stomach, hair spread around her, blood oozing out from her body, staining the carpet.

"Emma!" Who could have done this and why hadn't he heard anything? Staggering, he turned and made his way to the wall phone. "Police! There's been a murder!" He stammered out the details and let the phone go. Turning, he opened the back door and ran outside.

The police found him sitting on the gravel driveway. "Inside. She's in … in the living room." He clutched his arms around him, shivering.

"Get him a blanket," one of the detectives said to his constable. "We'll go and see what's happened."

A few minutes later the detectives returned. "I'm Detective Inspector Jason and this is Detective Jones. You're Joel Martin, aren't you?"

"Yes. Do … do you know what happened in there?"

"Not really, Mr Martin, but we remember you. You were here when your sister died, weren't you? Your parents had a hard time of it after that, coping with you, and then you disappearing on them."

"What's that got to do with this, Detective?" Joel stood up

angrily, shaking off the blanket. "What about the body in there? What about my Emma?"

"What body, Mr Martin? There isn't one."

Joel began to shake again as the detectives showed him the living room, completely normal and devoid of a body or blood stains.

"What's going on? What's happened?"

Emma ran into the room. "Joel, are you alright?"

"Who are you?" Detective Inspector Jason asked, turning to her.

"I'm Emma Dawson, Joel's partner. I've been shopping in town. We're here to sort out the house. What's going on?"

"Mr Martin phoned us and said there had been a murder, but there's no body. We'll have a look around while we're here but I think he needs to rest."

"Joel, come and sit down. Tell me what happened." Emma pulled him onto the sofa.

"I … I'm fine. I thought … I don't know what happened. I'm going up to rest." He pushed himself to his feet and left the room. She sat staring after him.

"He had some trauma in his young life. Coming back here after so long has probably brought everything back."

"Yes, I know about that. I'm sorry for all the trouble."

"Okay, but keep an eye on him. He may be in shock."

"I will."

"Joel, are you awake?" Emma sat down on the bed.

"Yes."

"Tell me what you saw?"

"A body. Lying on the living room floor. I thought it was you."

"You … you saw a body? But …"

"Now you think I'm mad. The police certainly do."

"I don't know what to think. Maybe it's what the detective said, you know, you've been through so much, and you're probably in some sort of shock right now."

"Really? Well, it's over now and I just want to get sorted and get out." He sat up, swung his feet over the side of the bed. "Coming to help?"

"Yes. I'll be down in a minute." She heard him going down the stairs and a few minutes later she heard a shout and he appeared at the bedroom door.

"The … the body is back! It's there again!" He stood, shaking.

"What! Let me see." Emma pushed past him and raced down the stairs into the living room. "Joel! Joel! Come down. There's no body here. What's happening to you?"

"There is, I tell you."

"No, there isn't. Look!"

"Bloody hell! What's going on? I just saw the same body again, I know I did." Joel put his hands to his head. "I am going mad, aren't I?"

"Come into the kitchen and I'll make some tea." Emma took his hand and led him to the adjoining room. "Sit down. We'll get through this, honey, don't worry."

"Yeah, right." He sat down then stood up again. "I need another look." He walked back to the living room. "No! No!"

Emma ran to him, put her arms around him. "Oh Joel, Joel. Come out of here. Come on, let's leave! Right now!"

"Go away! Let me go!" He pushed her aside and ran upstairs.

She heard a door slam.

Joel stood in the dim, musty interior of Margaret's room, shaking.

"It's alright," the whisper came. "Everything will be alright." The voice seemed to float around him.

"Margaret?"

"Yes. Don't worry, you're going to be alright."

"Margaret, I'm so sorry …"

"Ssshhh, Joel. It will be over soon."

He heard a noise and turned around as the window suddenly flew open. He felt soft hands on his back, propelling him towards the bright daylight outside.

"Don't worry, it will be all over soon." The hands were now firmer on his back and he found himself balancing on the window ledge. "No!"

Joel's body lay shattered, his eyes wide and staring, his blood a crimson cloak around him.

Footsteps

It was cold. And dark. The moon had retreated behind heavy clouds and rain fell silently as she walked quickly along the footpath. Her footsteps echoed in the empty street as she quickened her pace, pushed her hands deeper into her coat pockets.

She stopped. Silence.

She glanced behind her but all she saw was fog swirling in the ghostly shadows from the dim glow of the street lights. Pulling her collar higher around her neck and pushing her hands back into her pockets, she continued walking, but slowly this time. *Footsteps*! Someone was following her.

No, just someone else foolish enough to be out at this late hour. She should have caught a taxi, it would have been a lot safer. And she wouldn't be so wet either. But it did seem a ridiculous idea when she lived two streets away from the club. Oh why hadn't Adam picked her up as usual? Maybe it was him. She looked nervously back down the street. Nothing. No-one.

As she walked on she heard the footsteps again. When she slowed they also slowed and when she walked faster so did they. Yes, there was definitely someone following her. Who? What did he want? He? Maybe it was a she. Perhaps one of the girls from the club.

She stopped, and hearing nothing forced herself to look around again. No-one. But wasn't that someone standing over there? A black shadow in the murky light. No, just her imagination. But if it was her imagination, where was the person who was following her? Where was he hiding?

Suddenly frightened, she began to run. *Nearly home now.* But she could hear the footsteps. *Closer. Closer.* She could feel the closeness of someone behind her, hear his heavy breathing.

On trembling legs she stopped, panting. She turned and saw a large, dark shape looming over her. Screaming, she backed away until she felt the hard bricks of a wall behind her. Trapped. "Wh … what … do … you want?"

Something glinted in the pale light. Her eyes filled with terror as she saw the knife. Her scream echoed down the quiet street as it flashed towards her … …

"Cut! Well done, everybody. Take a break for lunch and we should wrap the movie this afternoon."

The Suit

The old man's arthritic fingers expertly guided the material beneath the rapid movements of the needle. He'd only ever had one suit in his life though he'd made hundreds for other people, but the suit he had made for his wedding all those years ago to his dear Maria had worn very well and what did he need two suits for anyway?

Ah Maria, I remember how beautiful you were in your white dress, with your lovely long black hair wound around your head. Oh bella, I wish you were still here and not lying cold in your grave. I'm tired of my life and very tired of my family – they're like vultures circling me, waiting to pick over my bones, and I fear that may be very soon. I'm so lonely without you and our little house is so empty.

He stopped sewing and stood, stooped and aching, his hands clutching the back of the chair for support. After a few moments he shuffled to the kitchen and poured a small glass of red wine which he took to the table where he sat heavily in a chair. He might be old but he still enjoyed his wine. And his independence. He didn't need anyone, he could manage very well on his own thank you. Tina could ask all she liked but he wasn't going to live with her, his grandchildren were far too noisy. How many now? Seven, yes and all still at home, lazy lot they were. That husband of hers should find a better job, they never had any money.

And Dominic, he was no better. He and his money were soon parted and his wife was the same, spending what they didn't have and teaching their four kids to do the same. But they'd never asked him to live with them, not that he would have. And neither had his youngest, Mario. At least he and Theresa only had three kids, but she was a funny one, quite cold and distant towards him. He didn't trust her one bit. They were all after his money, the money he'd saved for years. But that wasn't going to happen. It was well hidden.

Well, time to get back to his sewing. He needed to finish before he ran out of time. He sat back at the machine and continued until darkness crept into the room. Sighing, he stood and switched on the light then held up the jacket he'd just finished for inspection. Yes, perfect. Now he could start on the trousers. But in the morning. He was tired and hungry and feeling just a bit cross. He shouldn't think about his family, they always made him cross. He should only think about Maria.

The next morning, after a wedge of cheese and strong black coffee, he sat at the machine again. At least the trousers would be quicker to sew than the jacket. They didn't need lining. That had been very fiddly to do. But by the end of the day he would have his suit finished and possibly the shirt.

Later that night he sat on his bed and looked with tired eyes at the beautiful black suit hanging on its hanger in the wardrobe. A crisp white shirt hung underneath the jacket and a pair of shiny black shoes with black socks poked inside sat neatly beneath the trousers. What a job he had done. Possibly his best ever. But now he was ready. His suit was finished and waiting for him. And so was Maria.

In a tiny graveyard in the valley a group of people surrounded a coffin. As it was lowered into its waiting grave there were no tears, no regrets. There were sly smiles of anticipation as their time had come. Their mean, selfish father had finally succumbed to his illness and they could now get what was owing to them — what he had deprived them of all these years.

Their father, resplendent in his black suit, was lying safely inside the satin-lined box, a smile on his waxen lips.

The Dream

Last night she dreamed about the room again. Now, sitting at the kitchen table in her small apartment, Hannah stared into her coffee cup, the memory of the dream hovering over her so that awake or asleep she couldn't forget. It was strange. It was almost not a dream but a silent picture and she'd been having it for the last two weeks and each time the picture revealed something more, like a jigsaw being put together piece by piece. And each time she woke at 4 am.

Pushing her cup to one side she rose and went back to bed, but sleep evaded her. When the sun finally bathed the room in its golden glow, she pulled on a T-shirt and track pants and left the house to jog in the park, something she had enjoyed doing at sunrise most of her life.

While jogging, she tried to focus on her job as secretary at the medical centre and her duties for the day, but the dream once more intruded. She stopped and sat on a bench. Leaning on her elbows, her head in her hands, she saw the room in her dream, a large room with big armchairs full of cushions, a square rug on floor boards and a fire burning in the fireplace. A child with blonde curls sat on the rug, its back to Hannah. *Oh turn around, please turn around. How much longer before you turn so I can see your face? A week ago you weren't even there.*

Two nights later when she awoke at 4 am it was so close. So close. The child had almost turned, as if to look at her.

The following day at work Dr Masters called her into his office. "I'm worried about you, Hannah, you don't look well, so I'm going to send you on sick leave and I suggest you take yourself off somewhere and have a holiday. It's been a long time since you had one."

"Oh, are you sure, Tim? It's so busy here at the moment and there are an awful lot of files to clear."

"Don't worry, I'll get a temp in."

"Well thank you, I really appreciate it. I certainly could do with some time off."

"No problem. Take as long as you like."

Hannah smiled. Twenty-five years was a long time to have the same boss. She didn't like to think of working for anyone else, and at sixty years of age the job prospects probably weren't that great. She didn't want to let him down, but it was his suggestion and she was so tired. A few days off would be wonderful.

She contemplated her lonely life. No husband. No children. No family. Not even a lover. Just memories of an orphanage, happy memories actually, but as she'd been a sick child, thin and painfully shy, she'd had no best friends and almost no boyfriends. A photo was given to her while at the orphanage – of herself as a toddler with her parents in front of their house. The name Bennett Loop was written in ink on the back. But they had died when she was small and she had no memories. As there were no known relatives, there had only ever been herself and at her age she realised there would only ever be herself.

She was greeted by a grey drizzle when she left work so she stopped at a gourmet shop and bought some ravioli stuffed with mushrooms in a cream sauce. That would cheer her up and she'd have a glass of wine as well while she thought about how she would spend her leave.

At midnight, after falling asleep in front of the television, she finally dragged herself to bed. As the rain drummed on the roof and thunder rumbled in the distance she yawned. *Too tired to dream.* But at 4 am when the room was bright with lightning flashes and vibrating with thunder she suddenly sat up, her body quivering. She had dreamed. And this time she saw the child's face. It was the face in the photo. Her own!

Hannah switched on the bedside light and reached for her dressing gown. What was happening to her? Why was she always having the same dream? She ran downstairs into the kitchen. *Coffee.* She needed coffee. While the kettle boiled she pulled an old chocolate box out of a drawer in the dresser. Inside were the few treasures she'd collected over the years. Taking out the photo, she stared at the face of the child in her dream, her face, and at the timber house behind them with its big, odd-shaped chimney visible on one side. Apparently her parents had rented the house while her father worked in the local timber mill. All she knew of her family was staring up at her from the fading photo. That was her history.

Well, since she was now on sick leave she would pack some things, close her apartment and drive to Bennett Loop. She'd never been there before, never had a need to, but now she wanted answers. And something told her she would find them in that town.

The sun was shining in a clear blue sky when Hannah pulled up at the town's motel. After checking into her room and putting on sneakers for comfortable walking, she set out to explore. A few brightly painted shops, a post office, a small park with freshly mown grass and an elegant town hall occupied two streets which

were surrounded by timber houses. As she could hear the hum
of the timber mill in the distance she bought a Coke from the deli
and asked directions.

She soon found herself on the outskirts of town where the mill
sat at the base of a small hill. A few houses were dotted around
and a gravel road behind the mill disappeared through the bush
and up the hill. Sipping on her drink and trying to think above
the grinding noise of the saws, Hannah wondered what to do
next. All the houses she had seen had identical chimneys which
didn't look anything like the one in her photo. It was time to
show it to someone and hope they knew something.

Back at the deli she showed the photo to the girl behind the
counter, although the chances of her knowing anything were
slim. She was much too young. "I know it's a long shot but do
you recognise this house at all?"

"No, sorry. I've only been in town a few months, came with
my boyfriend when he got a job at the mill. I was lucky to get
work here, not much happening in this place."

"Thanks anyway. I probably need to speak to someone who's
lived here for a hundred years then."

"Yeah, right. Oh, there's an old guy lives at the boarding
house, retired or something. Comes in here for cigarettes. He
might be able to help you. It's in the next street."

"Thanks so much. I'll check him out." Hannah wandered off
along the footpath, suddenly enjoying the freedom of not
working and the warm sunshine which was making her quest
easier to deal with in this lovely little town.

The sprawling timber boarding house sat neatly behind a white
picket fence. A "For Sale" sign on a post had been hammered
into the lawn and red geraniums grew in terracotta pots along the

path to the red front door, which was open. "Hello, is anyone there?" Hannah poked her head inside. "Hello."

Soon she heard footsteps and a tall slim woman with grey hair piled on top of her head appeared.

"Can I help you?"

"Yes, I hope so. My name is Hannah and I need some information about a house. Here, this one in the photo. Do you know it?"

"No, love, can't say I do. But come through, someone else may be able to help you. I'm Joan. I run this place but I've only been here ten years."

"Oh, I was told by the girl at the deli that there was a man here who might know."

"She would have meant Eric. He's lived here a long time. Retired now but, as his wife is buried here, he didn't want to leave. He's my only permanent resident, the rest are mill workers who come and go, but have a seat and I'll go and find him."

Hannah settled into an armchair in the large lounge room. There were paintings and framed photographs of old timber workers all over the pale green walls while couches and chairs were arranged in front of a large TV. Little tables and lamps were scattered around the room, making it cosy and appealing. A large fireplace occupied a wall with the fire set ready to light and an old clock ticked away the time on the jarrah mantelpiece.

"Hannah, this is Eric. He's a little deaf so you'll have to shout a bit. I'll go and make us some tea." Joan helped Eric to a chair next to her and bustled out of the room.

"Hello Eric. Nice to meet you."

Eric smiled and nodded. A cloud of grey hair covered his head and bushy grey eyebrows hung over his watery blue eyes. "I don't get many visitors so it's nice to meet you too. What is it you need to know?"

"I'm trying to find out where this house is. I believe it's in this town somewhere and a part of my history." Hannah passed him the photo and waited for Eric to put on his glasses.

"This rings a bell." He tapped the photo with his finger. "Mmm, a long time ago, but it's the chimney. It's the chimney I recognise. Yes, the Jones house."

"That's my name. Jones." Hannah leaned forward eagerly. "So what do you remember?"

"You're a Jones? Did you live there?"

"Well, I think I did. This photo is all I have. My parents died and I was brought up in an orphanage. I have no memories of this house or town, so I … I've decided it's time to check out my past."

"Oh, well, it's not a good story I'm afraid. The house burnt down and the family were trapped inside."

"What? Oh God, that's terrible, but … but what do you mean 'the family'? I'm still here."

"I don't know everything – it happened before I came here. All I know is that at four o'clock one morning a fire burnt the house down before anyone could get there to help and the family couldn't get out, so I don't think you could have lived there or you wouldn't be here now."

"But … but I've always assumed the child in the photo is me and I'm with my parents. I've had it all my life."

"Well, love, I think you might have been given someone else's photo." Eric handed the photo back to Hannah and patted her hand as Joan arrived with a tray of tea and cake.

"Has Eric been able to help?" she asked, setting the tray on a side table and passing out cups.

"Thank you. Yes, but unfortunately I'm none the wiser as to my family history." Hannah sugared her tea and stirred. "I've always thought I was the little girl in the photo but now it seems I'm not."

"The chimney is still there," Eric said suddenly, spilling cake crumbs as he spoke. "I just remembered. The house was halfway up the hill at the back of the mill but the old brick chimney didn't burn down. It's still there as far as I know. Probably crumbling a bit now though."

"Oh. In that case I'll have a look while I'm in town. Thank you so much, Eric, you've been a great help. And thank you, Joan, for the tea, and your cake is delicious."

"No problem, Hannah," Joan smiled. "Come back again, the kettle is always on in this place. Although, I have to add, only while I'm here."

"You mean the For Sale sign at the front?"

"Yes, when I can sell this place I'm moving back to the city. It's where all my family are and as I'm now a widow I'd rather be closer to them, though I will miss it here. It's a nice place to live."

"It has a relaxed feel to it."

"It's a very laid-back town and on a gorgeous day like today we're all a bit lazy. No-one rushes here. Well, as I said, call in again. It's nice to have someone new to talk to."

The next morning Hannah woke at eight o'clock. She had slept all night without dreaming, the first time in ages. Was the jigsaw now complete? Was that it? She made herself a coffee while pondering. No, there had to be more. There had to be a reason for her dream. If she wasn't the girl in it then who was?

As it was another sunny day she put on her running clothes and jogged towards the mill.

There was a smell of burning sawdust in the air as she ran past the mill and up the gravel road. She could see a few houses through trees on each side of the road but mostly it seemed to be bush, then, as the road turned slightly, she spotted the chimney, just visible over the shrubbery.

She stopped and stared at it, her heart suddenly hammering in her chest. The remains of an old gravel driveway could be seen here and there underneath small plants and shrubs and the area in front of the chimney was covered in a tangle of creepers and small trees.

Hannah made her way through and stood in front of the crumbling ruin. *Now what?* She felt nothing. No connection, but it was eerie knowing a family had died here. Falling to her knees she sighed and felt tears stinging her eyes. What was she supposed to do now?

Above her, she heard kookaburras laughing. *Appropriate.* The whole thing was laughable.

Vines, which were entwined through the bricks, appeared to be preventing the chimney from disintegrating completely, and tiny plants sprouted from the cracks. From her crouched position she suddenly noticed something inside the blackened fireplace, protruding from the side wall.

She scraped at the bricks until she could get a good grip on it and pulled. A small, dented tin box fell out of its hiding place in a little cloud of dust. *Well, how long has the chimney been keeping this secret?* Hannah tugged at the lid until it flew open on rusted hinges, revealing a tattered, yellowing book. Its thin faded pages fluttered in the breeze as she stared in amazement.

As she gently lifted it from the box she saw something else. A locket, the silver tarnished and marked, lay curled underneath. Putting down the book, she picked up the locket and as she did so dizziness overcame her and the day disappeared into blackness.

Was she dreaming again or was this real? She was in her dream, sitting on a rug in front of a crackling fire. She looked around. There was a woman sitting in an armchair, knitting, a man seated at a table, writing, and on the rug next to her was another child. Herself. *Oh God! A twin!* She was a twin! Her parents looked down at them and smiled.

Then Hannah was back in front of the chimney, the locket in her hands, and staring up at her were the faces of two identical babies. She put the book and locket into the tin and walked slowly back to the motel, trying to figure out what had just happened to her.

Propped up on her pillows, her feet tucked under her, Hannah carefully opened the book. Some of the pages were illegible but they revealed enough of the story she so longed to know. Her mother was Italian, her father English, and they were living in the city. As they were about to move to the country for her father to begin a new job in a timber mill her mother gave birth to twin girls prematurely. One baby was not expected to live and remained in hospital while her distressed parents took the other baby to their new home.

Hannah's father decided to keep a diary of their daily life for the baby they had left behind as a positive action in believing they would one day bring her home. As her mother had not fully recovered from the birth and didn't speak English fluently she seldom left the house, consequently most people in the town never knew she had a sick baby in the city as well as Helen, her healthy baby. And as she was terrified of bushfires they had kept the diary behind a brick in the fireplace.

Tears streamed down Hannah's cheeks as she read the last entry:

This diary is for you Hannah, because we know that one day you will come home to us and you will be healthy and you will read what our life is like in this town without you, our darling daughter. Your mother is terrified of bushfires which seem to occur frequently around here so we are keeping this book, and a locket for you, amongst the only bricks in the house. Hopefully the safest place.

So the fire her mother feared had prevented Hannah ever coming to live with her family. *Oh Helen, why have you waited so long, all these years, to come to me in a dream? I have been so alone.*

Hannah picked up the locket and stared at the tiny photo. *Why didn't you come before?*

"Time means nothing here, Hannah. Now, is important for you. One day we will all be together and you will understand." The soft voice seemed to fill the room. "I have shown you your family and your past. You will have a happy future." The voice began to fade. "Happiness is yours for the taking, Hannah."

"Helen, don't go! Please stay." But there was silence. Hannah sat still on the bed, her mind whirling. *A happy future? Where?* Her tiny apartment and job at the medical centre were her world. But she couldn't say she was really happy, she just did what she had to do. She'd never considered anything else.

The dream had started all this. Thinking about her life and wanting to know her history. Now she knew. The jigsaw pieces had finally revealed the picture. And left her feeling unsettled.

Did she want to go back to the city, to her home and job? Or could she do something different? Was there something else for her? She was certainly enjoying not being at work at the moment, just driving here and checking into a motel was all very carefree and not at all like her.

Helen had shown her the way. She was sure about that. But what way? Well, she would sleep on it and think about it tomorrow.

After her early morning jog Hannah stopped at the deli which she happily discovered had a small breakfast menu. Freshly squeezed orange juice, eggs – free range of course – and home-made bread as well as coffee served in a small plunger.

She sat at a table out the front, enjoying yet another beautiful sunny day, and contemplated her future. As she finished her coffee it suddenly came to her. *Now where did that idea come from?*

Pushing back her chair she walked off toward the boarding house. A cup of tea with Joan. And a chat. And her jigsaw would really be complete.

Parallel

It had been one hell of a day at work and was now going to be one hell of a night, with traffic at a standstill, rain sleeting down and me going nowhere fast. Could things get any worse?

As I sat watching the windscreen wipers flick backwards and forwards and failing miserably to keep the rain off the windows I reflected how much like my life they were. Here I am, going backwards and forwards to work and failing miserably.

My marriage failed when my husband disappeared with my best friend and my job was about to end. They call it redundancy. I call it bad luck for me. Not even a decent pay-out. Which means with no job I won't be able to afford my rent and I'll have to move house. The only thing in my favour is there are no children. Thank goodness. Just me to worry about.

As the cars in front of me began to crawl once more through the cold wet night a plan began to form in my mind. With no family, no job, no house and nobody to worry about why did I have to stay in the city? I'm a journalist. I can get a job anywhere. Even in another country. Hopefully. Maybe it was time to take that trip to England to see Uncle Arthur. My Dad's brother had been asking me for years to visit him and his wife, Aunt Maud, but she had passed away and he was on his own as they had never had children. There was really nothing to keep me here anymore.

A few weeks later found me at the Portsmouth train station

with two suitcases and a backpack. I found a taxi and gave the driver the address in Southsea as my uncle said he wasn't well enough to drive. It wasn't far and we soon pulled up outside a semi-detached house with a low brick wall in front and a tiny paved area behind with some pot plants that had definitely seen better days.

I trundled my cases to the front door and knocked with the old lion's head knocker. I heard footsteps and the door opened to reveal a stooped man with a bush of grey hair above a pale, lined face. He was wearing a dressing gown and slippers.

"Hello, Uncle Arthur. I'm Ella," I put my arms around him. "It's so lovely to finally meet you after all these years."

"Ella my dear, lovely to meet you too. I've been looking forward to this and I'm so sorry I'm not well, but it's just a cold. I'll be up and about soon, but come in, come in." He led me down a hallway into a small sitting room filled with bright sunlight that was streaming through the French windows. I put my cases down and looked around. "What a gorgeous room."

"Yes, I haven't touched it since Maud passed away. It's just how she liked it. But sit down, I've got the kettle boiling. Would you like tea?"

"Yes, thank you, Uncle. Can I help?"

"No, I can manage; make yourself at home. I'll take you upstairs later."

The room was painted cream with a pale blue sofa and matching arm chairs. Yellow curtains at the windows fluttered in a soft breeze. Blue and yellow cushions were lying in a heap at one end of the sofa and two books were on the other end. A small coffee table was littered with newspapers and more books and a TV was on with the sound turned down. Through the windows I could see a small neglected garden with red roses and daffodils bravely flowering along the dividing wall to the house next door. At the end of the garden was some sort of structure that looked like half a water tank. Maybe it housed chooks, or chickens as he would call them. I turned when I heard him behind me. "Would you mind moving those papers, dear, so I can put the tray down."

"Of course." I shuffled them to one side and took the tray from him. "These cups are beautiful," I said as I noticed their lovely patterns.

"Maud's of course. She always used them for visitors but I don't get many. Now, sugar, milk? And I made you some toast in case you're hungry."

"Thank you, I am a bit peckish actually." And so my uncle and I got to know one another over tea and toast and then he showed me to my room upstairs. He had given me the large front room which faced the busy street below.

"I've moved to the small room as this one is too big for me now."

"Oh that's so nice of you. I'm just happy to be here, it's been such an awful year."

"I know it has, dear, but I want you to stay with me for as long as you like, treat my house as your own. It will be good to have the company."

As my uncle spent the following week recovering I walked the streets, familiarising myself with the neighbourhood. It was a very busy area with shops, restaurants, churches, a large park and a bus service into Portsmouth and I loved it.

At the end of the week I decided that my holiday was over and

I should find a job. But my bad luck hadn't deserted me as there were no vacancies for a journalist anywhere, not even on the local paper. Another week passed and I decided that maybe I should try my hand at waitressing or washing dishes in a restaurant. My uncle's failing health didn't help my mood either.

Uncle Arthur had reluctantly retreated to his bed as his condition was worse so I took over the cooking and cleaning, in between job hunting. "I'm so sorry I can't show you around, introduce you to people, but don't worry, Ella, things will work out," he told me.

But I wasn't confident. I was worried that he had more than a heavy cold. I had planned on moving to London if I couldn't find work around Portsmouth but I couldn't leave him while he was so sick and I really did feel comfortable in his house.

One afternoon I took a cup of tea and a book into the garden. It was a glorious sunny day and I sat on the old stone seat which I'd found when I did some weeding and sweeping. It was hidden underneath an overgrown shrub next to the half-tank structure, which uncle told me was an air-raid shelter that they had never bothered to remove. So, no chooks but something far more fascinating.

As I sat drinking my tea I looked at the shelter whose entrance was almost blocked by the shrub but I could see a rusty iron gate with a broken lock. Curiosity got the better of me and I pushed it open. A flight of stone steps led down into dusty darkness. Not to be deterred I pulled my phone from my pocket and switched on the torch.

There were only a dozen or so steps before I reached the bottom where there was a large space with wooden seats and a box of candles and two lamps on a small table. How terrifying it must have been to hide in here while bullets flew above creating all sorts of damage. It was so damp and musty. The floor was compacted earth while the walls and ceiling were made of wood. Some earth drifted through the cracks and a couple of roots dangled above me.

I tentatively sat on a seat and looked around, caught up in the atmosphere of this secret hiding place. Then I saw the door. It was partly concealed by a cupboard but on inspection I saw that it was made of iron and firmly closed with a lock that was still intact. Well, I was sure that my uncle would offer an explanation.

That evening after I had taken his dinner up to him, I sat on the edge of the bed and asked him to tell me about the shelter. "Did you go down there?" he asked between mouthfuls. "How did you get in?"

"Well, the lock was broken so I thought I'd have a look. As you can imagine I've never been in an air-raid shelter before and I'm quite fascinated by the idea. Did you really go down there during the war?"

"Yes, but I put a lock on it years ago. It's quite dangerous — the roof could fall in at any time."

"I suppose so, but I was wondering … Uncle, there is another door which is locked and partly hidden behind a cupboard. What's behind it?"

"Nothing. Nothing at all."

"Nothing? That's surprising considering it is made of iron and locked."

"Ella, please don't go down there again, it's dangerous and I don't want anything to happen to you. Now I think I need some rest. Thank you for dinner, it's nice that you are cooking for me."

"No problem. I'll take your tray down." But I was glad he

didn't make me promise not to go back into the shelter because I was even more curious about that door.

The next afternoon, while Uncle was sleeping, I went back to the shelter with a crowbar that I had found in a toolbox under the sink. With some difficulty I managed to move the cupboard and break the lock, but opening such a heavy door wasn't easy either. After a lot of pulling it slowly opened to reveal stone steps leading down into a tunnel. Well, I had come this far so I thought I may as well see where it led.

The tunnel was quite long and very dark even with my torch, but eventually I was confronted by another iron door, this time without a lock. Was this some sort of escape route that maybe led to the sea, which wasn't far from Uncle's house? I never thought in my wildest dreams that I would have such an adventure.

I pushed on the door and as it creaked open I couldn't believe my eyes when I found myself back in the shelter.

As I stood there pondering, the outside door opened and I saw myself enter. Yes. Myself! Tall and slim but with her dark hair piled on top of her head instead of loose as mine was. *I must be dreaming, this is impossible.*

"Am I awake?" I asked. "Or is this a dream?"

"You're not dreaming. You've crossed over."

"Crossed over? Crossed where?"

"My name is Eva. What's yours?"

"Ella. But … … but you look like me. What's happening?"

"I think you need to sit down, Ella. I'll explain. You walked through the tunnel and crossed over into my world."

"Your world?" I sat down at the table. This was too much.

"Yes, a parallel world to yours."

"What! That's fantasy stuff, it's impossible. There's no such thing as a parallel world. I've just left my uncle sleeping and walked through a tunnel, gone in a circle and come back to where I started, though I can't explain you. It's weird, like I've suddenly split in two. You are joking, right?"

"No, I'm not. Everyone in your world has a twin in mine. Even the buildings. As one is built here so one is built in your world and vice versa. But there are connections, or portals, between our worlds through some sort gravitational manipulation but they usually remain sealed. Occasionally someone from your world or mine crosses over by accident, as you have just done. Scientists have all sorts of theories but we think there was some kind of glitch in the universe which created a sort of mirror world to yours. The same, but not the same. Things will look familiar to you but in an odd sort of way."

"That's a load of rubbish!"

"No, it's not. How do you explain me? Our uncles built their shelters at the same time and they inadvertently found the portal between our worlds. They believe that there are many portals which haven't been discovered and some that have which governments keep top secret. We can't afford for our worlds to publicly know about each other. It would be catastrophic."

"So Uncle Arthur knew about this. No wonder he warned me. He said it was dangerous to come down here."

"He was right. He and your aunt used to secretly meet my aunt and uncle on a regular basis until my uncle became ill and they locked the doors. You should never have opened that door."

"I'm a curious sort of person. I couldn't help it. Can I see outside?"

"Yes, it is similar to yours I'm told, but we need to be careful in case my neighbours see us."

Once through the door I could see we were back in the garden. It *was* similar, but not the same. There was a table and chairs on a paved area, a small patch of lawn and a row of shrubs along the dividing wall. The house looked the same. "Wow! This is incredible! Do you live here, Eve?"

"Yes, with Uncle Fred. I'm not married. Well, I was. Once."

"Me too. You don't have an Australian accent like me. Where are you from?"

"Here. I've never been to Australia. And I've never crossed over to your world either but Uncle Fred told me about it years ago."

"Do people ever cross over and stay?"

"I don't know. It's possible I suppose."

"Wow again! This is so unbelievable! Here I am in another world, talking to my twin."

"I know it's a lot to get your head around. Uncle Fred has told me so much and until now I've kept it secret. You and I know so much about each other and yet we have only just met."

"Yes, as I said, it's unbelievable. Is … is your uncle's wife alive?"

"No, she died a few years ago and I have been taking care of him since."

"My aunty died also, but your uncle … is he still not well?"

"He's dying I'm afraid. And … … and so will yours soon. Apparently they live and die at the same time so everything stays balanced."

"Oh, poor Uncle Arthur. I must get back to check on him. He

might be awake and wondering where I am. I've moved here from Australia and now I'm looking after him."

"There is a small time difference between us, so he may still be sleeping. Ella … .could … could we meet again?"

"Yes, I would love that, we have so much to talk about. We could take up where our uncles left off."

"I think they would like that, but now I'll take you back to the tunnel so I can lock the door again. Make sure you lock yours too."

Back in my world I ran up the stairs to Uncle's room just as he was waking. "How are you feeling? Can I get you something?"

"A cup of tea would be nice, dear." He struggled to sit up so I piled the pillows behind him and handed him his glasses and book.

"I'll be right back. Don't go away." I smiled at him as I left the room. When I returned with our tea and some cake I had made earlier I confessed what I had done in the shelter. He stopped eating and looked at me in disbelief.

"I told you not to go there," he said sternly. "I really didn't expect you to go against my wishes."

"But, Uncle, it turned out okay in the end. Eva is really nice and we got along so well."

"I'm sure you did. So did her uncle and I, but it's fraught with danger. If anyone finds out what you are doing you will be in serious trouble. Both of you."

"But you managed all these years without anyone knowing."

"Yes, and with nosy neighbours I don't know how we kept it secret. Please, Ella, reconsider what you're planning to do."

"For the last few years my life has been going nowhere. I feel like I'm a mouse in a wheel going around and around. I had a husband, a house, a job and a best friend and now I have none. Things are different here. You're my family and I feel like I belong and suddenly I'm in the middle of an amazing adventure and I'm really happy. "

"Ella, my dear, I have so loved having you here with me. You're like a breath of fresh air coming through and helping me with everything. You are so much like your father with your sense of adventure. I don't really blame you for going into the shelter. He would have done the same. He was always into mischief."

"I'll stay here and look after you as long as you want me to."

"Unfortunately that won't be for long. I'm dying, Ella."

Eva's words rang in my ears. Her uncle was dying. So mine was too. I burst into tears.

"Don't cry, dear. I've had a good life and a lot of luck. I've left everything to you."

"Oh, Uncle Arthur." I put my arms around him as the tears streamed down my face. "Thank you so much. I never expected that."

"You've been my sole beneficiary for years, Ella. We have shared some wonderful letters and I certainly don't have anyone else to leave my house or my old car to. You have proved to be as lovely in real life as you sounded in your letters. But dear, Eve's Uncle Fred is also dying so maybe it's just as well you have met. If you can manage to keep your secret you and she will be great friends, just as Fred and I have, and our wives when they were alive. But you must fix the locks on those doors yourself if you can. Nobody else must go in there."

"Thank you again, Uncle. And I am sorry I disobeyed you but

my curiosity got the better of me."

"I understand. Maybe you should be a writer. You could write about parallel worlds. Now wouldn't *that* make a story!"

"Mmm, yes, there's a thought." I smiled. "A complete work of fiction though."

About the Author

Ten Pound Pom, June Kingston Smith, lives in Perth. Her storytelling is universal with an engaging and intriguing narrative. She often writes of the connection that some of us have (and perhaps sometimes may not want to have) between our present and past lives.

With a knack for magnifying the incidental, her many published travel articles and restaurant reviews – a far cry from her natural talent with telling tales of the supernatural – still capture a spirited and descriptive style and it's this distinctive writing that has awarded her The Society of Women Writers (WA) Bronze Quill for *In Another Place*, and first place in the ITC Australian Pacific Region fiction writing for *The Diary*.